The Way Back

by

Linda LaRoque

The Way Back

Published by *L.G. Smith Books*
Cover Art by *Diana Carlile*

Publishing History
First Edition, 2011
Digital ISBN 978-0-9893792-4-3
Print ISBN 978-0-9893792-5-0

Published in the United States of America

Acknowledgements

Have you ever wanted to travel back in time? I have. Not to live forever, but to explore the time period and see what cities and rural areas looked like before the growth of today. Wouldn't it be a treat to travel Route 66 in its hay day, wear the clothing and the hair styles of the period? History is fascinating and the events of our past are fodder for wonderful stories.

Research is a great excuse to travel. Fortunately for me, Kilgore, Texas, the setting for *The Way Back*, isn't far from where I live. I'd been there many years ago but felt the need to return to refresh my memory and visit the East Texas Oil Museum. If you're ever in the area, stop in and tour the museum. With its reconstructed street scene, it's a step back in time to the 1930s.

Writing *The Way Back* allowed me to experience the hardships of the stock market crash and the trials of life in the Texas oil fields. As much as the time period intrigues me, I prefer to live these events vicariously, through reading and writing. I hope you enjoy Amber and Wellman's story.

Listed below are the references used to construct this story.

Eason, Al, BOOM TOWN: KILGORE, TEXAS, East
Texas Oil Museum Kilgore College, 2005
http://www.depotmuseum.com/oilBoom.html
http://www.easttexasoilmuseum.com
http://www.forttours.com/pages/kilgore.asp
http://www.onlinenevada.org/articles/reno-divorce-
colony-literature
http://www.texasranger.org/dispatch/18/Beverly%20Tu
cker/Tucker.htm
Godfrey, Cullen M. "Mike", A BRIEF HISTORY OF
THE OIL AND GAS PRACTICE IN TEXAS, Texas
Bar Journal, October 2005
www.texasbar.com
http://txgenes.com/TXGregg/OilField.html
http://www.thepeoplehistory.com/1932.html
http://en.wikipedia.org/wiki/Women_in_the_workforce

One

New York City, February, present day.

Goodbye, Gram. Give my love to Mama and Daddy.

Fat snowflakes danced in the breezy air, landing on her face and hooded coat. Her heart was as cold as the frozen ground of the white covered cemetery. The preacher and other mourners waited. Amber Mathis made herself move, stepped forward, and laid a long-stemmed red rose atop her grandmother's casket. Turning away, she swiped at the tears trailing down her face.

Her grandmother's suffering was over. The two-year battle with cancer had been slow and agonizing. Without medical insurance other than Medicare, Amber was determined the dying woman have the best care possible. She'd worked like a fanatic to pay for a full-time private nurse when she couldn't be there.

Few people were here today as she laid Gram to rest. A couple neighbors, her secretary, and several others who worked in her office building were the only attendants.

Now they surged toward her. She braced herself.

Accepting their condolences with nods and a whispered "Thank you," she locked her knees and stiffened her spine to keep from crumbling. She wanted to escape and be alone with her abruptly altered existence. What would she do with her life now? Busy caring for her grandmother and making money, she had few friends. They hadn't called in months because they knew Amber wouldn't leave her grandmother's side except to go to work.

Now, she was all alone with a job she dreaded—a job that left her little or no time for a life. In the next week or so, she'd settle her affairs and look elsewhere for work. She was tired of dressing up, fancy dinners with clients, and the ever present fear of letting a client down. Maybe she'd wait tables for a while to get her head on straight. It would be hard work, but less demanding. All she'd have to worry about would be getting the person's order right. She might just sit around and do nothing. Her bank account wasn't depleted and would support her for several months, longer if she economized.

At last everyone left and she slipped into the cab that waited. The warm air felt wonderful to her icy hands and feet, but her teeth chattered and shudders racked her body.

"I can turn the heat up, Miss Mathis, if you want," said the burly cab driver as they exited the cemetery and shot out into the traffic filled expressway leading to town.

"Thanks, Joe, but I'll be fine in a minute."

An hour later, he pulled the cab into a vacant spot in front of the Hathaway Building downtown and jumped out to open her door. She handed him two twenties. He made a point of answering her calls first, and she tipped him generously.

He thanked her and added, "Real sorry about your

grandmother, but at least she's not hurting anymore."

"Thank you, Joe. You're right. She's at peace." And Amber knew she was. The pain towards the end had been unbearable, to the point they'd kept her sedated most of the time. It was a waste of their last hours together but Amber couldn't stand watching her suffer.

She passed through the revolving door of the five-story office building. At one time, the Hathaway Bank had occupied the bottom and top floors. The ones in between had been leased as all five were today. Her heels clicked against the large marble tiles of green and black that led her down the hall to the pair of elevators. Green marble covered the lower half of the walls, polished mahogany the top. Crystal chandeliers hung from the twelve-foot ceilings and small fan shaped sconces hung on the walls. She loved this old building with its Art Deco feel.

Inside the elevator car, she pushed the button for the fifth floor and started removing her gloves and hood. The lights flickered and then went out, the car lurched, and she lost her balance. She fell back landing on her butt. "Well, hell," she muttered as in the dark she bent her legs sideways in the straight skirt and, groping for the handrail, scrambled to her knees.

Before she could pull herself up, the lights came on. An elderly man in a gray uniform loomed above her, clasped her elbows, and lifted her. "Here, let me help you up, ma'am. I'm right sorry. This elevator has been cranky the last week. Mr. Hathaway had someone from Otis Company in to look at it early this morning. Guess they'll have to come back."

Amber could only stare. The man hadn't been on

the elevator when she stepped inside, had he? Could he have been in a corner and she didn't see him?

"Who are you?" Her eyes flashed around the compartment looking for other passengers she might have missed. There were none. "How'd you get in this elevator?" She wasn't afraid. He didn't appear to be a threat and had instantly released her after helping her up.

"Why, I'm James. I've been operating this elevator for the past fifteen years." He chuckled. "You scared me to pieces. I didn't know I had a passenger until you hit the floor. I was just giving this contraption another test drive."

The elevator stopped, and she noticed the hand on the dial above the door was on the number five. *Dial? Where was the digital readout? How...retro!* How come she'd never noticed that gadget before? Then James pulled a gate back from the door before it slid open. Goosebumps broke out on her skin and the nape of her neck tingled. Gates on elevators had been replaced before she was born. Gran had mistrusted these new versions, convinced that without gates, if the doors opened accidentally, she'd fall down the shaft. Was she in the wrong building?

"This is the Hathaway Building, right?" she asked.

"It sure is." He peered at her closely. "Are you all right? I can get you some water if you want."

"No, no, I'm fine." *I think.* "Thank you for the ride up. I'll probably be here until nine or so."

His wrinkled brow furrowed even more. "You work here?"

She nodded and extended her hand. "Amber Mathis."

He shook it enthusiastically. "Well, well. This must be your first day because I've never seen you before." He tipped his cap. "Hope you'll be happy here, Miss. Sure a surprise that Mr. Hathaway's hired another secretary. After the bust, he had to let people go to pay his depositors."

A secretary? How trite was that? She'd thought even the older generation was past putting people in categories. Should she blister his ears and tell him she was an investment banker? Nah, let him think what he wanted. Anyway, she found another aspect of his comment more interesting. A Mr. Hathaway had never worked in this building in the five years she'd been here. What bust was he talking about?

She strode down the hall and stopped in front of her office door. Instead of solid wood, the upper part of the door was an opaque glass. Stenciled on it were the words *Wellman Hathaway, President & CEO Hathaway National Bank.*

What the hell? The Hathaway Bank had moved from this Hathaway Building years ago, so what explained the CEO suddenly having an office here? Not only that, in the space she considered her office.

Breath coming in rapid gasps, she reached for the doorknob and turned it. The door opened easily, and she walked into a plush office with a large oriental rug in front of a huge mahogany desk. Facing the desk was a sitting area with a large brown leather sofa, two matching chairs and a coffee table decorated with a wood sculpture. She wasn't an expert on art, but the paintings hanging on the wall didn't appear to be the mass-produced kind.

Nothing in the room looked like the things in her

office. Could she be on the wrong floor, in the wrong building? No, Joe wouldn't drop her at the wrong address, and she was tired and distraught, but not so much so that she'd not recognize the building where she worked. Of course, in the hallway, she'd noticed on an almost subconscious level that everything did look newer, brighter.

On shaky legs she walked toward the massive desk and the gold calendar holder between the two pen sets with inkwells. *Inkwells? Good grief, they were real.* She could see one had black ink and the other, red. Hand shaking she braced herself on the edge of the desk and leaned forward to see the date. She lurched back, accidentally knocking the piece to the carpet. *Holy shit! February 25, 1930?*

Knees trembling she backed up and plopped down into a chair. Her heart thundered in her chest, and she struggled to slow her breathing. *Close your eyes. This is a dream. You'll wake up in a minute, and everything will be back to normal. Please, God, let it be so.* Her head resting on the back of the chair, she counted slowly as she took air in through her nose and blew it out her mouth.

She peeked through one eyelid and squeezed it shut again when nothing in the room had changed. February 1930. James had mentioned the big bust. Said Mr. Hathaway had been laying off staff and trying to pay his depositors.

Did he mean the stock market crash of October 29, 1929?

Okay, there has to be a reasonable explanation. There's no such thing as time travel. She didn't believe in ghosts, UFOs, or any of that other hocus pocus crap.

The only answer was she'd lost her mind. The stress and pressure of her job and caring for her grandmother had been too much.

A loud cough broke her trance. For the first time, she noticed the room was cool. What used to be a plate glass window was now a large walnut framed window, wide open. A tall man stood on the ledge just outside. The opened sash hit just below his shoulders as he leaned back against it. Legs spread, hands clasped behind his back, he transferred his weight from one foot to the other.

Dear God. He's going to jump. She'd read about the stock market crash of 1929 and how many men had thrown themselves off tall buildings rather than face poverty, their families, or the people whose dreams they'd crushed.

He muttered something that sounded like a curse. She couldn't sit there and let him jump—take his life. Could she talk him in off the ledge? Not likely. He thought he was alone. If she spoke up, her voice might scare him and cause him to fall prematurely. *Prematurely? Amber, you've gone nuts.* Maybe not. Perhaps she'd been put here for a purpose—to save him from jumping. Worrying her bottom lip with her teeth, she made up her mind. Easing from the chair, she approached as quietly as she could. As she stood behind him, she felt the heat emanate from his body and could smell his spicy cologne. This was no dream.

Stop him! Do it! In one swift move she locked her arms around his waist, pulled, and dropped to the floor. She cringed at the loud crack when his head hit the window sash as he fell back, landing on top of her.

They both remained still for a moment. The air

knocked out of her, she managed to gasp out, "Could you move? You're squashing me."

He rolled and her head bounced on the floor as she changed positions from trying to rise to flat on her back. Long arms held hers above her head and muscled legs kept her body from moving. Striking gray eyes pierced hers, examining every inch of her. Her face flushed at the intrusion and she struggled to get him off. He applied more pressure and she stilled.

A lock of blond hair fell over his forehead, a patrician nose flared in anger, as his square jaw tightened. He ground out, "Who the hell are you and why'd you try to knock my head off?"

~*~

Wellman Hathaway sat at his desk and stared out the window at the New York City skyscrapers. He was finished. He'd liquidated as many of his assets as possible and paid his bank depositors on the halves. Guilt ate at his soul over not being able to pay them in full, but he'd done what he could. Most had been satisfied, understanding it was the best he could do. Others hadn't been so accepting. A few were downright violent. He still sported the bruise on his chin from Mr. Samuelson's fist.

He sighed in disgust. He couldn't blame them. They had families to feed, no jobs, and now no money. That'd make any man violent. Many of his associates hadn't been able to handle the stress and had taken their lives. How could they leave their wives and children to fend for themselves?

In that respect he was lucky, he supposed. Madeline had divorced him two years ago and had remarried. Unfortunately her husband was one of those who'd jumped from the roof of his Wall Street office building. Now Madeline struggled alone to keep some small part of her former existence alive.

He was better off than some. He owned this building and his home. That knowledge was all that kept him sane. But there would be no buyers for either one. No one had liquid assets to buy property. No, that wasn't true. A few people who hadn't kept their wealth tied up had money and were buying property for one-third its value.

If necessary, he'd sell the family art to keep his wheelchair bound father in their home until he could find a way to recoup his losses. His depositors would be paid in full or he'd die trying.

Rising, he stretched, popping his back. He needed some fresh air. The radiators kept the room either too hot or too cold. He strode to the tall window and raised it. Snow covered the two-foot ledge. He wiped it away with his hands and, as was his habit when needing a breather, he ducked and stepped outside. It was wide enough where he felt at ease standing. There wasn't enough room to try any shenanigans, but he didn't plan on being stupid.

The air was cold. Large snowflakes hit him and melted. Below the streets were turning to a nasty brown slush. He better try to leave for home within the hour or the roads might freeze. His Packard handled slick roads well but one little slip and he could land in a ditch. Walking several miles in this weather would be punishing.

He took in a deep breath. Frigid moisture hit his lungs making him cough. "Damnation!" Foolish action on his part. *Breathe through your nose unless you want to catch pneumonia.*

Suddenly he was jerked from behind, his body folding in half, his head cracking on the window sash as he went down, landing on a body. Stunned, his ears ringing from the blow to the back of his head, he remained still.

A voice from below him said, "Could you move? You're squashing me."

His survival instinct ignored the ache of his head and within a second he had flipped to his front and had a small person trapped beneath him. The gentle curves under him identified his attacker as a woman before his eyes took inventory of his prisoner. Legs, as long as snow skis, were bare from her high-heeled shoes up to a number of inches above her knees. She wore a long sleeved black suit jacket to match the skirt and a long hooded coat of the same color lay spread beneath her.

By the time his eyes reached hers, her creamy skin was flushed dark red. She hissed and bucked beneath him. He increased the pressure of his legs on hers and continued to stare at the riot of her hair. How else could he describe the short mess on top of her head? It was dark, almost black and would be beautiful if it had any order to it, but it was spiky all over. Still, she was beautiful, and his body responded to her softness, the subtle scent of perfume wafting from her skin.

He shook himself. What the hell was he doing perusing her hairstyle, enjoying her fragrance? *Fool!*

He growled, "Who the hell are you and why'd you try to knock my head off?"

Her mouth opened and closed like a fish. First woman he'd ever met at a loss for words. She sputtered. "Get off me, you jackass. I was trying to save your life, keep you from jumping off that ledge."

Jackass? Hmmm, was she telling the truth? Probably. There'd been enough jumpers the last few months. He released her and rose to his feet offering her a hand as he did so. "I wasn't jumping, just enjoying a little fresh air."

She ignored his hand and wiggled her way to her feet in the short tight skirt.

"Yeah, right. What kind of idiot steps out a ledge five stories up to freeze his ears off?" She tugged her coat around her, obviously chilled by the room's coolness.

As he closed and locked the window, he conceded to himself it probably looked odd to an outsider, but he'd done it for years and some days it helped to clear his mind.

He turned back to see her staring around the room, a look of desperation on her face.

"Did you come in to see me, Miss…?" he asked. He extended his hand. "I'm Wellman Hathaway. If you're in need of a loan, I'm afraid we're fresh out of money." He'd meant the comment to make her smile, but if he wasn't mistaken, she was near to tears.

"Here, here, now. Whatever is wrong, it can't be that bad."

"It *is* that bad! I buried my grandmother this afternoon at two o'clock and returned here to finalize a few things." She turned her pained blue eyes on him.

His heart twisted. "I am so sorry, but what things do you need to finalize here? Was your grandmother a client of ours?"

"No. My office is in this building. My name is Amber Mathis. I'm an investment banker here."

"An investment banker? Now that, I find impossible to believe. Miss, I know everyone who works in this building and certainly have no investment bankers on staff. Especially not a woman."

"But I *am* one. When I got on the elevator, it lurched and threw me to the floor. A man was there operating it and a gate covered the door. Gates were done away with ages ago—sometime around 1950, I think, so naturally I was confused."

Wellman thought she must be still confused. "Let me get us a cup of coffee and you can tell me all about it." Fortunately the coffee was still hot from the pot he'd brewed earlier. He did enjoy his coffee break in the afternoon. He glanced toward his guest. "Sugar or cream?"

"No, just black."

He returned and handed her a cup and sat in the chair adjacent to the sofa.

No gates on elevator doors? 1950? What the hell was she talking about?

"I got off the elevator then I came in here," she went on. "This should be my office but it's all changed."

Wellman set his cup and saucer on the coffee table. Concern inched up his spine. Another poor misplaced soul had lost her mind over the terrible depression. He guessed he should call the police. They'd know how to get her help.

"I don't know what I'm going to do," she said. With her cup in hand she rose and walked to the window to stare down on the busy street. "I'd hoped I was in the wrong office, the wrong building, but even the street below is different."

He cleared his throat. The unfortunate woman, her misery made him uncomfortable. She was so pretty, except for that hair, it was a shame, such a waste. "Miss Mathis, I'll call someone to come help you." He rose and started toward the phone on his desk.

She turned. "That's just it. No one can help me." Her face pale, she walked toward him. "I know this sounds mad, so crazy I hate to say it out loud." She took a deep breath. "Mr. Hathaway, I fear I've traveled back in time."

Oh Lord, she really is nuts.

She pointed his desk calendar lying on the Persian rug. "The date says February 25, 1930, but when I walked into this building, it was February 25, 2011."

Two

The man looked at her as if she'd sprouted an extra head. His sympathetic expression changed to one of disgust. Full lips tightened into a straight line, he stepped back from her as if she had the plague. She stifled the urge to laugh, gave up and giggled her way to the coffee pot to refill her cup. Cup clattering as she walked and chuckled, she made her way to the sofa and sat down. *Lord, she was going crazy.*

He picked up the phone, dialed zero, and growled, "Give me the police."

She lost it. Bent at the waist, she felt laughter roll up and out of her. Coffee spilled on the tabletop as she tried to set her cup down. Unable to stop, she waved her hands and howled, "Please…wait…oh, Lord, maybe I *am* nuts." She wiped tears off her cheeks with the backs of her hands. "Let…let me explain a few things before you have me thrown into a padded cell."

His gray eyes pierced her, one eyebrow cocked. Saying "Never mind," into the phone, he returned the earpiece to its cradle and moved to the chair furthest from her and sat, posture rigid. Damn, he was a good-looking man, but a mite skinny for her tastes. Oh, there was muscle under that fine wool suit, no doubt about that, but she liked her men beefy.

"I'm waiting. You have exactly ten minutes," he said.

"Okay, okay, I'm a bit hysterical as you can see. It's been a bitch of a day." She opened her large handbag, removed her driver's license and handed it to him.

He read it front and back, and then returned it. "A good likeness, but it could easily be a fake. Just because it says your birth year is 1980 doesn't make it so. I'm afraid you'll have to do better than that, Miss Mathis."

She tossed him her cell phone. He caught it and raised that brow again.

"Open it," she muttered, frustrated he could be so glib about her evidence. He fiddled with it until he figured out how it opened. "It's a cell phone, a telephone that is portable. In 2011 I can call all over the world and hear just fine."

Suspicious gaze flicking between her and the phone, he studied it then asked, "If it's a telephone, where is the dial?"

"You press the number you want to call, tapping each button in sequence."

He in punched in some numbers. When nothing happened he snapped it shut and tossed it back to her. "So much for your proof," he said. "It didn't work."

She wanted to scream, but took a deep breath and explained succinctly. "Of course it doesn't. There are no cell towers in 1930. They operate on radio signals, but there are none in this time period."

"Harrumph. Likely story." He waved his hand. "Continue with your fantasy."

"All right, smart ass, take a look at this." She handed him her PDA.

He bristled. "I don't like your attitude, Miss Mathis, or your vulgar vocabulary. I would suggest you

15

curb you crudities if you want me to consider your *proof.*"

She wanted to lash out in frustration, but decided she best do as he asked. Squelching her panic, she muttered, "All right. I apologize."

"Apology accepted. Now, show me how this contraption works."

A surge of hope rushed through her at his interest in her PDA. She moved to stand behind him, giving directions over his shoulder. Like a little boy, he tried out each of the games and reviewed each of its functions before handing it back to her.

She returned to the sofa. Eyes serious, he studied her with concern. "I still can't accept the fact you're from the future," he said. "But, I can recognize that something very strange has occurred. I'll help you in any way I can."

Amber's throat clogged with emotion. Her voice broke. "Thank you. I can't tell you how much better your support makes me feel. If it's worth anything, I can't believe what's happened to me either. I keep thinking I'll wake any minute in a hospital with a head wound or something."

She opened her wallet. "Here, I have probably close to a thousand dollars. That should see me through until I can find my way back. Can you recommend a good hotel?"

He took one of the bills, studied the date, and felt its texture. "I'm afraid you'd be arrested for counterfeiting." He handed the money back to her. "I don't have much cash, but I can offer you a place to stay until we find you a job and a place of your own."

Her chin trembled, she bit her bottom lip to keep

from sobbing and making a fool of herself. "Thank you, Mr. Hathaway. I'll find a way to repay you."

He avoided looking at her, cleared his throat, and muttered, "I'm sure you will, but we'll not worry about it right now. With your credentials, though it will be hard to get anyone to believe you're an investment banker without documentation of some kind, I'm sure there will be many individuals who can use your expertise."

The door flew open and crashed against the wall. Wellman jumped up. "What the hell?" he shouted.

Six men, led by Mr. Samuelson filed into the room. Samuelson carried a baseball bat. Grinning, he said, "Well, well, don't have money to pay us but you've got money to hire a classy *secretary*?" He snickered.

"Now, see here, Samuelson, your tone is insulting and you need to apologize to the lady. She also has lost all her funds and hoped I could loan her money."

Samuelson snorted. "By the looks of her clothes, she seems to be doing all right."

"Don't be an idiot, man. What does clothing have to do with anything? Your wardrobe hasn't suffered either. Can't you see she's been crying and is distraught?"

The burly man studied the woman who now stood at his side, face pale with concern, cheeks still damp. "Beggin' your pardon, Miss," he stammered.

Wellman knew the man was honorable, just desperate and from the looks of his companions he wasn't keeping good company.

A skinny little man pushed his way to Samuelson's side. "Get on with it, Bud. We didn't come here to exchange pleasantries."

Samuelson nodded. "That's right. Mr. Hathaway, we came to leave you a little reminder of what you owe us, something to carry with you all the time." He turned to the group. "Get him boys."

Wellman had knocked two out cold before the others had him on the floor in a headlock. He could hear Miss Mathis screaming and a man cursing. He roared and tried to get up only to have a knee jammed in his kidney. "Don't hurt her," he choked out. "I'll kill you if you do. She has nothing to do with this."

"Appears to me you're not able to do anything right now, but after we break a few of your bones, you'll be able to do even less," said Samuelson.

Wellman threw all his energy into trying to dislodge the men, but they held on tight. One pulled his left hand away from his body. His disgruntled depositor lifted the bat and aimed at his hand. Skinny man pushed him aside and took a shortened sledgehammer from his coat. No telling what he had in the other side because now the dirty garment almost reached the ground. "Here, let me do it with this. Get the job done faster. Starting with the pinkie, right?" asked the creep.

Without waiting for an answer, the man smashed the hammer onto his finger, bone cracked. Wellman threw back his head, his scream echoed off the wall. The tendons stood out on his neck threatening to make his head burst. He renewed his struggle, gasping for air, cursing. "Son-of-a-bitch. I'll get…you…Samuelson."

"Hold him tight boys. One more ought to do it."

Held flat to the floor, he waited for the hammer to fall. A high-pitched shriek split the air. "You stupid jackasses, let him up."

More yells, grunts, and howls echoed around the

room in unison with Miss Mathis's screeches of fury. Whoever was holding her must have turned her loose because she knelt at his side and turned her wrath on Skinny and Samuelson. "Don't you have an ounce of sense? If you do more injury to him, he'll not be able to work to pay you back. And believe it or not, his intention is to regain his fortune and return your money to you."

"Sure, lady," growled Skinny. "Tell us another fairy tale." He shoved her, she sprawled on her back and by luck, swung her right leg, catching him under the chin. He fell back like a rock, out cold.

In an instant she was beside Wellman again slapping at the men who held him. "Get off him. Move, you oaf." She and Samuelson helped him stand and eased him into a chair.

Samuelson asked. "Is he really planning to pay us back?"

"Of course he is. We both are."

Wellman tensed, his thinking hazy. What was she talking about?

One of the other men interrupted. "She's lying, Bud. Just trying to save her boyfriend's pretty hands. Don't listen to her."

"I beg your pardon, sir. I'll have you know I'm an investment banker and specialize in situations like the stock market crash. Mr. Hathaway and I are partners."

Regaining his voice, Wellman sputtered, "Wait just a—"

She clapped her hand over his mouth. "Darling, we can tell them. I don't mind that you're marrying me for my money." Before he could utter another word, she kissed him square on the lips. Not a hasty one but one that said shut up and listen. When she released him, she whispered against his mouth. "Trust me."

Too stunned to speak, he merely nodded.

She smiled and continued her lecture to the wide-eyed men. "In nine months, I'll come into a large sum of money—money that's been hidden in the ground until I come of age." She took a deep breath and batted her eyes at him. "You see, my folks don't trust banks, so they buried it to keep it safe."

Mumbles rolled around the room. "Smart thinking."

"Sensible folks."

"Wish I'd a thought of it."

Samuelson's expression was serious and not completely believing of the story. He asked, "When's the wedding."

Miss Mathis blushed, as well she should after telling such a bald-faced lie. She coughed. "Why, we haven't set a date yet."

"Well, I have," said Samuelson.

Wellman cringed, knowing where the man's mind was headed. He watched him walk to the coat rack and grab his coat. He came back. "Your coat, Mr. Hathaway. It's a short walk down the street to the church. A Protestant church agreeable with you, Miss Mathis?"

"Why, why, yes, but please gentlemen, I'd rather arrange my wedding myself. You know, white dress, flowers, and all."

"Afraid that won't do. I want this knot tied tight tonight so I'll know Mr. Hathaway won't duck out on you after the money is in his hands."

"Now see here," Wellman bellowed. How dare

they insinuate he'd be anything but honorable? Marry this woman? He couldn't do that. He didn't even know her. His hand throbbing, he ground out, "Samuelson…you can't force us to get married."

"No, but I can break a few more fingers to convince you if necessary. You might be able to stand the pain but I don't think the little lady here could. She appears to be rather sweet on you."

~*~

Amber hoped she'd step off the elevator alone and be back in 2011. When it didn't happen, she pinned her desires on the door. To her dismay, vintage cars lined the streets, some parked, and others moving as large snowflakes fell. Neon signs topped buildings and hung in windows advertising businesses and indicating whether opened or closed. If her situation hadn't been so dire, so weird, she'd have enjoyed the scene before her, but it wasn't to be. Their escorts hustled them down the street to a large church on the corner. Inside they said their vows, were handed a piece of paper, which Samuelson confiscated for safekeeping, and were hustled back to Wellman's car with a final warning.

"I expect to see you nine months hence with our money," said Samuelson. "Is that clear?"

"Crystal," growled Hathaway.

He turned his back on the men, took her arm, and helped her inside his car. He rounded the hood, slid behind the wheel and the powerful engine roared to life.

That had been thirty minutes ago, and Mr. Hathaway hadn't said one word. Not that she blamed him. Not only did he have a busted finger, but he had a wife he didn't want. If that wasn't enough, he was now on a deadline to pay his debtors.

Why had she come up with that money buried in the ground idea? Getting married? She'd been desperate and grappling for anything to keep them from hitting him again, that's how. The oil boom in Texas just popped into her head and she winged it. She shuddered. The sound of the bone in his finger cracking wouldn't be forgotten.

She glanced at his stoic, silent profile. Well, two could play at that game. She snuggled into the plush leather seat of the Packard and closed her eyes. How could she have known the men would force them to marry? What was the big deal anyway? It would be easy enough to get a divorce.

She must have dozed because the car had stopped and Mr. Hathaway held her arm as he helped her from the vehicle. They stood in a circular drive in front of a large Tudor home. Lights blazed in the downstairs windows. Small ground lights outlined the sidewalk and led the way to the well lit porch.

"Your home is beautiful, Mr. Hathaway," she said as they started walking.

"Well, it appears it's your home now, too, for a time at least." He fixed her with a stare. "I think in front of father we should drop our formality and call each other by our first names."

"Oh yes, I agree." She stopped in mid stride. "Look, I'm sorry about the wedding. We can get a divorce as soon as you want, but I just couldn't let them continue to hurt you."

"Wouldn't it have been enough to say we were partners?"

She didn't have a clue what had prompted her to say they were getting married.

"And to say I was marrying you for your money…that's the most humiliating of remarks. I'd never marry for money."

"I was just trying to prove how honorable you were, how much you wanted to pay your debts and clear your bank."

He studied her from his greater height. The top of her head reached his shoulders even in her high heels. "How do you know I'm honorable? I could be the worst scoundrel in the state."

"Instinct," she said. "I'm a good judge of people. Anyone who tried to pay his depositors back, even if it was on the halves, when he could've used the money himself, is a principled man."

Arm around her shoulder, he started them walking again.

"You know," she said, "in the future, the FDIC insures bank depositors for up to $250,000."

"What is the FDIC?"

"It's the Federal Deposit Insurance Corporation. If available today, it would have lessened the blow considerably. The stock market crash is what prompted the government to initiate the insurance in 1933."

Face serious, he said, "I don't know how much to believe of what you say."

"I have no reason to lie. I'll prove to you somehow I'm telling the truth."

He opened the front door and they stepped into a wide hallway beautifully furnished with round center table holding an enormous floral arrangement. Antique chairs, a sofa, and end tables lined each side yet left plenty of room keeping it open and gracious.

An elderly woman dressed in a black uniform

rushed into the hall from the back of the house. "Mr. Wellman. We were beginning to worry."

Wellman handed her his coat and helped Amber remove hers. "Hattie, this is my wife, Amber Mathis Hathaway."

Hattie was clearly stunned but quickly suppressed her surprise. "How do you do, ma'am." She nodded toward a room across the hall. "Your father is waiting for you, sir."

"If you'll take Mrs. Hathaway upstairs to my bedroom so she can freshen up, I'll go in and give Father the news." He kissed her on the cheek, for Hattie's sake she was sure. "Go on. I'll be up shortly."

His bedroom? Well, gee, they'd not had a chance to discuss their living arrangements but she was surprised he'd install her in his bedroom. Evidently he didn't want Hattie to know the nature of their marriage.

On the second story landing they turned right. Halfway down the hall, the housekeeper opened a door and stood back for her to enter. The room was huge. The bed was king sized, the headboard and posts dark mahogany. At the end sat a chaise, the deep maroon and gold matching the spread and draperies. A large chifferobe stood on one wall and a fancy ladies dressing table with a three-way mirror occupied the opposing wall.

The woman noticed her admiring it.

"It belonged to his first wife. Guess he was too sentimental to get rid of it," she said, a look of smug satisfaction on her face.

Hattie bustled into the bathroom. "I hope you find everything in here you need. If not, let me know and I'll find it for you."

24

"Thank you, Hattie."

"Dinner is at eight and formal."

Amber merely nodded. The woman didn't like her. She knew she'd arrived without a suitcase and wanted to make her feel uncomfortable. We'll, she'd picked on the wrong country bumpkin. She'd walk in to dinner any damn way she pleased.

Then again, maybe she'd skip dinner. She wasn't sure she wanted to meet Mr. Hathaway Senior. Right now Wellman was telling his father her story and how they'd come to marry. *Oh God, will he pitch me out on my ear? Into the cold?* Wellman wasn't completely convinced of her story. She couldn't imagine what his father would think.

Three

The minute Wellman escorted Amber into the dining room, his father, waiting in front of the fireplace, rolled his chair forward to meet her. "Father, this is Amber. Amber, my father, William Hathaway. This crusty old man has quite a bark, but I assure you he's harmless."

At his words, the tension left Amber's shoulders and she smiled. "How do you do, sir?"

"I couldn't be better."

Wellman hid his smile at the goofy grin on the old man's face. His father longed for this to be a real marriage, wanted grandchildren, but it wasn't going to happen. Not with this woman anyway. She was too attractive. He wanted an undemanding wife he could care for, one to raise his children and make appearances when he needed a hostess. This woman would not only demand a man's heart, she'd want his soul too. Plus, she was career minded and wouldn't be happy sitting at home.

William reached for her hands. "Bend down and let me have a good look at you."

She did as he asked and the old man chuckled. "She's just as pretty as you said, son." He clasped her face and planted a kiss on each of her cheeks. "Welcome to our family."

"Thank you, but..." Face flushed, she glanced from

his father to him for help.

Wellman patted her shoulder. "Don't worry. I explained the whole thing to him," he said. At least he'd tried. Hell if he understood everything himself.

Still in possession of her hand, Father placed it on his shoulder and rolled toward the long dining table. He pulled a chair out for her next to the end. "That's right. And regardless of whether he believes your story or not, young woman, I do."

Wellman pushed her chair in and moved to the chair across from her as his father took up residence at the head of the table.

Amber's expression brightened. "You do? You really believe I traveled back in time?"

"Indeed I do. Met a fellow once in that very building, who claimed to have come from 2003. As a matter of fact, it was the same floor. Said my office was his, that he was a private investigator. Oh, that was probably eighteen years ago, before you graduated college, son."

"So you said, Father." Tonight was the first time he'd heard about it, but when he mentioned Amber's elevator story, the old man couldn't wait to fill him in on the time traveler he'd met.

"Really? Is he still around? What's he doing?" asked Amber.

"No, from what one of the bank tellers told me, he was so agitated he ran out in front of a trolley, got hit, and was taken off to a hospital. We never heard from him again."

The swinging door from the kitchen opened and Hattie came in with a tray to serve the first course. Wellman wanted to chortle as his father frowned in mock irritation. "Now Hattie, you'll not be repeating one word of what you hear tonight. Do you understand me?"

She stopped, the bowl of soup suspended in front of him. "Have I ever betrayed your confidence, Mr. Hathaway?" She set the dish down and turned to serve Amber and returned to the tray for Wellman's dish. "No, I haven't and you know it so don't be issuing orders needlessly."

"Harrumph. Well, just so we're straight," Dad muttered.

"Straight as a string," she muttered as she picked up the serving tray and marched out through the swinging doors.

"He had one of those cell phones like Wellman said you have," the old man said in between tastes of soup. "Now, he didn't have one of those PDA things. I can't wait to see it. It has games on it, you say?"

"Yes, sir. It does. I'll bring it down for you after dinner with the charger in case the battery runs low." She bowed her head and then looked up eyes glittering with tears. "I've been so afraid you wouldn't believe me, would think I was crazy and toss me out in the street."

His father patted her hand. "Now, now. None of that. I believe you. You've been through a mighty unusual experience and I don't doubt I'd be at a loss under the circumstance. Don't worry. We'll not let you go through this alone." He turned his eyes on Wellman. "Will we, son?"

"No, sir, we won't. Put your mind at ease, Amber." He had nothing against helping the woman. Marrying her was something else all together, but what was done, was done. For the time being, at least.

Her smile lit the room. "Thank you."

Wellman sat back and listened to them, enjoying their interchange. His wife was an unusual woman, not cold as Madeline had been. From an old established New York family, Madeline made sure everyone was aware of her pedigree, something offensive to his father, whose father was a self-made man. Tall and pencil thin, her dark auburn finger-waved hair, Madeline turned heads. When she'd honored him with her attention—perhaps because he was wealthy, he'd thought it was his charm and shining character.

Father had never approved of her and yet he welcomed Amber with open arms. Was it possible she'd been sent specifically to help him in this time of need? It was a nice thought, but unrealistic. Such didn't happen except in fairy tales. And if it was so, what did she have to gain from this venture?

He studied her as she talked. Blue eyes alight with intelligence and interest sparkled in the candlelight. She wore one of Madeline's discarded dresses and looked much better in it than his ex-wife had. Of navy satin, the shift style was sleeveless and showed off her lovely arms. The neckline dipped low giving him an ample view of her creamy breasts. Her dark hair, tamed to look less spiky, glowed with health. His body lurched in appreciation, but it was the warmth she exuded that drew him. How the hell would he be able to keep his hands off her while sharing the same bed? But, he wouldn't have her staying in another bedroom. He could always slake his lust with any number of females, but that idea was unappealing. They were married; they'd sleep together, and if she were willing, they'd have a sexual relationship for as long this adventure took. Otherwise, he'd remain celibate. He didn't intend to fall in love with her though. Madeline had taught him a valuable lesson.

Hattie removed their soup and served the next course. Father and Amber chatted like old friends. It was nice to see him so animated. Being confined to the wheelchair depressed him. Maybe Amber's presence would take his mind off his failing health.

Texas? Had Amber said Texas? He sat up straighter in his chair and listened to their exchange.

His father sputtered. "All the oil in Texas has been tapped. It'd be a waste of time to travel that far. Surely you know of some other means of getting rich quick. Something closer to home."

"No, sir, I do not," said Amber. "In early October of 1930 there will be the biggest oil discovery yet in East Texas. Wellman and I need to get to Kilgore and settle in. Then we can find a wildcatter with a spot in mind and the equipment needed to drill."

"Really, Amber, how can you know this?" Wellman asked. If she truly was an investment banker, he knew she had to be smart, but... "How can your memory be that accurate?"

"I remember because in high school I did a report for economics on the Daisy Bradford Number Three in Kilgore. About a month later, H. L. Hunt brought in another well north of the Bradford farm that produced twenty-two thousand gallons of oil a day. Come to find out it was the largest pocket of oil in the world. The town's population jumped from seven hundred to ten thousand in less than a month. People drilled everywhere. Even downtown. Eventually over a thousand wooden oil derricks lined the town's streets." She rubbed her forehead. "Darn, I wish I could remember the name of the old man who drilled that first gusher in the downtown area. He's the one we need to hook up with. He's already in his seventies."

The largest? And her knowledge came from 2011. Wouldn't it be wonderful to make money that easily, bet on such a sure thing? It all sounded too easy. "If the oil is downtown, how would a person go about getting a lease?"

"You'd find someone with vacant lots downtown and strike a deal for an oil lease." She laughed and her face grew more animated with each word. "If I remember correctly, someone drilled a hole right through the floor in one of the buildings on Main Street to get to the stuff."

"The main issue would be finding the right wildcatter. Darn, that man's name is on the tip of my tongue. Maybe it will come to me." Her hands moved, emphasizing her words. "We've got to get busy and get there fast, though. Before someone beats us to it."

"I thought you said no one knew about it."

"Well, I don't think they do, but there could be other time travelers with the same idea in mind or for that matter, someone could suspect it's there and be getting ready to drill, looking for investors, land to lease."

"I think she's right, son, but from what I've read in the papers, these oil towns are dangerous places. Not exactly the place for a lady." He turned to Amber. "I think you should let Wellman go by himself."

"Not on your life. I'm going and that's that." She stuck her chin out. "Anyway, the town isn't dangerous, it's the oil sites and where the roughnecks hang out that will be hazardous."

"Now, wait a minute, no one has said we'd try this venture. And Father's right, Amber. You wouldn't be safe there."

"Look," said Amber. "I'm bringing information to the table, that knowledge is my investment. You two will have to find the money we need to lease and drill, so you'll be our second investor, and the wildcatter has the equipment so he'll be our third."

She had a point. He looked at his father. "The only way I know to raise the money is to sell some of our art. Do you have any other ideas?"

Father rolled his chair back from the table and started for the door. "Come on into my study. Let's talk there."

The room was spacious, bookshelves lined the dark wood walls, and a large desk held pride of place. Two chairs sat in front of the antique wood piece, a large sofa with its back to the chairs faced a fireplace. Wellman had always enjoyed this room. As a child he'd read here while his father worked.

"You two have a seat," his father ordered as he rolled to the safe hidden in the bookshelf behind him. A set of shelves swung out, exposing the plate iron depository. He quickly ran through the combination. The door opened and he pulled a large leather folder out and turned, placing it on the desk. "This should be enough money to pay for your travels and let you drill a well. It's forty thousand dollars I put by years ago for just such a time as this."

Wellman couldn't believe it. "Father, you mean you had this money all along and I could have used it to pay our depositors?" He was sporting a broken finger when he could have paid all their debts and avoided Samuelson's thugs. "I can't believe you'd hold money back from people who need it."

"We need it too, son. Yes, we're better off than others, but life is not always fair. I'd intended for us to use this money to live on until we could get back on our feet, but with Amber's idea, it might be much sooner."

"And while we're off looking for oil, how will you live, how will you pay Hattie and the few other servants we have?"

"Don't you worry about that. We have the rents coming in from the building."

"Father, you know more than half of them won't be able to pay."

"We'll make it, son. If we have to, we'll turn this big rambling place into a boarding house."

~*~

It was set. They were going to Texas. Amber was so excited she couldn't relax in the big bed. Hattie had found her a nightgown, one of those slinky things they wore in the old days. It felt good next to her skin and slipped nicely against the sheets when she turned over but the tiny straps kept falling. She'd much prefer to have a T-shirt to sleep in.

Wellman lay with his back to her, a good fourteen inches between them. Before they'd gotten in bed, he'd given her his take on their marriage. "I would like a physical relationship but won't pressure you. I'll be faithful, care for you, but I won't fall in love nor do I want you to love me."

She could only gape at him and muttered, "I wouldn't dream of it, you jackass."

He'd snorted. "Call me names if you desire when we're alone, but never in public." Steely gray eyes pierced her. "Do you understand me?"

She saluted, "Yes, sir, master."

"Don't mock me, Amber. I mean it."

Rather than answer him, she'd turned her back and slipped between the sheets.

Now, here she lay, unable to sleep, worried about her future. Thinking that as soon as she got rich, she'd divorce Wellman's sorry ass made her feel better, and she relaxed. She'd almost dozed when she remembered her grandmother and the lonely grave in 2011. Grief rolled up into her throat and she stifled her weeping with her fist. Had it just been this morning? And how could she have forgotten her loss until now? *Fool, you've had a lot on your mind all afternoon and evening. That's how.*

Her grandmother, Martha Goldstein Mathis, had been eighty years old. In another week, she'd have been eighty-one. March fourth. Amber drew her knees up to her chest and sobbed softly. Gram had remained firm in her conviction. She was ready to die, to join Amber's grandfather in heaven, sit down with Jesus and have a little chit chat. A watery giggle escaped her. *Ah, Gram, if only I had your courage.* The humor lasted but a moment. Longing deep in her heart to be able to lay her head on her grandmother's breast again, feel her comforting arms around her, and wail out her loneliness overwhelmed her.

~*~

Wellman had been waiting to hear Amber's even breathing before he allowed exhaustion to overtake him. This had been one hell of a day. His finger throbbed. Though Samuelson and his thugs put a splint on it and taped it up nicely before the wedding, it still hurt like the devil. He'd downed a couple of aspirin with a serving of whiskey. Maybe they'd kick in soon. Hell, the picture of Amber in that silky white gown caused an ache elsewhere. The woman was beyond beautiful.

Ah, she'd stopped fidgeting at last. He allowed his body to relax and felt the bed shake. Soft sniffles reached his ears. *Ah, hell. Please, no tears. I'm just too tired to deal with them.* He was tired? How about her? Look what she'd had to deal with. She'd been plopped down in a different time period.

He rolled over and touched her shoulder. She froze and he pulled back

"I know this is all foreign to you, but things will work out."

"You don't even believe I'm from the future. You're just humoring me."

Well, he hadn't this afternoon, but his father's confession had convinced him. He cleared his throat. "I believe you now."

"Really?" she asked.

"Yes, really. Now relax and go to sleep."

She sniffed and her voice squeaked. "Okay."

He'd almost dozed when the bed shook again. "Dammit to hell, now what are you crying about?"

"My grandmother...I miss my grandmother."

Oh, God. How could I have forgotten this woman laid her grandmother to rest earlier in the day?

He gently clasped her arm. "Come here."

She slapped his hand. "I don't want your sympathy."

35

"I'm sorry. She must have been a wonderful woman for you to love her so."

"She…she was the…best." She sniffed. "She was all I had. She raised me after my parents died in a car crash when I was five. Gram held my world together."

Ah, hell. She'd suffered so much at such a young age. At least he'd had his father.

"She raised me with an iron hand but lots of love."

"What wonderful recollections you must have then, hmm? Try to think about those."

"Yeah, I do," she said, and then started to cry in earnest.

He remembered how broken he'd been when his mother died. Of course, he'd just been twelve, but no matter the age, it was a hard blow. "Ah hell, this is killing me." He touched her shoulder. "Come here." At first he thought she'd refuse, but in one swift movement, she rolled toward him and buried her face against his bare chest, an arm clutching at his waist, a leg lodged between his. He rubbed her back and talked softly as she sobbed, her body shuddering.

"You know, you're lucky to have had your grandmother so long. She got to see you grow into womanhood." He bent to kiss the top of her head then stopped himself. *Don't get carried away, now.* "I never knew my grandparents."

Her closeness was driving him crazy. His erection throbbed out the same rhythm as did his finger. Could she feel him?

Like a rocket, she jerked up in bed.

She looked down at him and choked out. "My grandmother will be born next Tuesday, March 4, 1930." She stared off into space. "I'll be alive when my grandmother is born. Is that weird or what?"

It was unbelievable to be sure. "Yes, definitely bizarre."

"Do you think there is any way I could find my great-grandparents and see her? I won't tell them who I am or anything, just make up some excuse why I wanted to see them."

"I don't see why not." He couldn't think of a reason to deny her. If it gave her some small means of comfort, then she should have it.

On a sigh, she lay back down and curled against him getting as close as she could. There was no way she couldn't realize how aroused he was. To his total shock, she squeezed closer to him and kissed his chest. He could feel her pebbled nipples against his chest and almost groaned.

"Thank you, Wellman. You're a nice man, not as much of a jackass as I thought."

"Don't jump to conclusions. You haven't known me a full day yet," he said, a grin curling his lips.

"Well, I do have to admit you're rather stodgy."

Him dull? He didn't think so.

"Yeah, I bet it'd shock your socks off if I kissed you right now."

"My dear, I'm not wearing—"

She stopped his speech with her lips. His shock didn't last long. Before she could break contact, he grabbed her head and deepened the kiss. Her lips were soft, hot, giving and taking as they moved against his. Her groan against his mouth fired the ache in his loins. He released her lips and trailed kisses down her neck and across her collarbone.

His flesh lurched in response to her gasp of

pleasure. The throb left his finger and centered in his groin. He growled, "If you want to stop, now is the time to say so."

"I don't want to stop. Do you?"

"Hell no, I want you, my dear."

To his surprise, she was as eager as he. Within seconds they were both naked and he relished the feel of her smooth skin against his, under his hands and mouth. That she explored his body with as much exuberance as he did hers, that she wasn't shy touching him, tasting him, made it impossible to distance himself from her. He slid one hand down her back and cupped her bottom, then moved with single minded intent around her hip to slide between her legs.

His fingers found her core wet, ready to receive him. She moaned and arched into his hand when he stroked the velvet folds. Unable to hold back longer, he turned her onto her back, spread her legs with his knees and positioned himself. In one smooth thrust, he entered, her body accepting him like a welcoming haven. He thrilled at the warm, clenching sensation, one foreign to his experience with Madeline in this bed.

Amber was on fire. Her body cried out with need. When Wellman entered her, her body thrummed, welcoming him as it had no other. He froze and dropped his forehead to hers, his breathing ragged. Her hands clasped his waist as he hovered above her, enjoying the feel of their joining, the blood and sensations running through her flesh. He started to move slowly then, and she met his every thrust. His pace increased and with her legs around his waist she arched against him. Far too soon, her climax seized her. She clung to him, riding the waves as he withdrew and drove in deeper still. He ground himself against her, starting the spasms of another climax. With their bodies arching in a frenzied dance of need, they reached their peak as one. They held each other tightly as their sweaty bodies trembled in the aftermath. Gasping for air, he rolled to his back taking her with him.

Amber lay in Wellman's arms. She nuzzled his chest with her nose, the soft hair tickling, and kissed him. He cupped her breast and thumbed her nipple. She struggled to keep her eyes open and yawned. Her hand ran down his muscled back and captured a taut buttock. Who would have known such a deliciously muscled body was hidden under that wool suit? It was one she hoped to enjoy as often as possible. Who knew sex could be so good without love? He didn't have to love her. She could handle respect, companionship, and good sex. The hard part would be protecting her heart.

He kissed her chastely. "Sleep, sweetheart, before you tempt me to take you again. We've got a lot to do in the next few weeks."

Four

Wellman stood at the end of the bed and watched his wife sleep. That mop of hair of hers stood up all around her head. It should detract from her attractiveness, but instead made her look like an enchanting elf. And, if he wasn't careful, she'd wiggle that cute little bottom of hers right into his heart. She was a passionate lover, one who could easily become habit forming. Last night as she'd lain limp in his arms while he gently stroked her back, a wave of tenderness had washed over him. It wasn't a welcome feeling, and one he must control. The woman was dangerous. He needed to keep up his defenses, not let her become necessary in his life. Never again would he let a woman control his heart and play him for a fool as Madeline had.

He reached down, grabbed a foot, and tugged. "Get up, sleepy head. We've got a lot to do today."

She bolted up in bed, clasping the sheet to cover her nakedness. Confused she looked around the room and then up at him. "It wasn't a dream, was it? I'm living in 1930."

"No, I'm afraid not." He walked to the closet and took one of his robes off the hanger. "Here. Slip into this and come down to breakfast. We can make plans while we eat."

~*~

Amber looked around in awe as she stood in the newly renovated Macy's store in Herald Square. The fully transparent showcases she was familiar with were gone, in their place dark oak cases with glass windows. The wooden escalators, some still in existence in 2011, were a novelty item for many of the customers, especially the children. She chuckled as boys rode them up and down as their mother's scolded their antics.

Hand at her back, Wellman prodded her toward the elevator. Inside, he said to the attendant, "Ladies Apparel."

They'd been on the floor less than a minute before a sales clerk joined them. "Can I help you?" The tall brunette eyed Amber's outfit critically and eyebrow cocked, turned to Wellman. "Something more stylish for the lady?"

Amber spoke up. How dare the woman treat her as if she were invisible? "The lady would like to see some jeans."

Evidently jeans weren't a common item for women in the 1930's so Amber settled for wool slacks and blouses. Wellman insisted she buy shoes, a suit, several dresses, gloves, and a big floppy brimmed hat. She felt ridiculous in the thing but at least it covered the slicked down hairstyle she'd received at the beauty salon. The stylist had exclaimed in horror over her uneven hair lengths, but when she finished, bragged to the other beauty operators and called the results, "Chic," she said, "very modish, madam."

When Amber was dressed in her stylish new suit with heels to match, they found seats in the dining room, the very one Macy's closed in 1998. The curved serving counters prevented customers from sitting in groups. It was a treat for Amber, seeing the Art Deco décor and living a part of history. She ordered a BLT and coffee. Wellman had the lunch special. She'd never been a fan of meatloaf.

Amber couldn't help admiring her reflection in the mirrors as they walked through the cosmetic section. She looked like a different person. She'd worn hats on occasion, but nothing like the wide brim felt creation that reached her shoulder in the back and turned down on one side and up on the other. As they passed the perfume counter, a variety of glorious scents wafted around them.

They'd almost reached the exit door when a feminine voice, chimed, "Wellman, Wellman, is that you?"

Amber stopped and turned, waiting for Wellman to do the same and speak to the tall attractive brunette behind the makeup display who'd called out to him. When she looked up, his face was a frozen mask. For a minute she thought he'd continue out the door, but he exhaled, his shoulders relaxing, took her arm, and escorted her back toward the cosmetic counter.

"It is you," trilled the woman.

Wellman removed his hat and nodded. "Madeline."

Ah, the ex-wife thought Amber. The bitch! She put her arm around Wellman's waist and snuggled into his side. His body was tense enough to break. "Aren't you going to introduce us, dear?"

He looked down at her in surprise. She fluttered her eyelashes at him. A hint of a smile twitched his lips and his face regained some of its color. "Of course, sweetheart. Madeline, I'd like you to meet my wife, Amber. Amber, this is my ex-wife, Madeline Peterson."

Madeline's fake smile evaporated. "Your wife? I didn't know you were seeing anyone."

He chuckled and Amber cut in. "We met yesterday. It was love at first sight. Before we knew what was happening we were standing before a preacher. As a matter of fact, we didn't have time to even buy rings. We're on our way to Cartier to pick them out now."

Madeline gaped. For a second Amber felt sorry for the woman, but darn it, she'd treated Wellman badly. Well, considering his reaction to seeing her, she assumed so.

Wellman cleared his throat. "I apologize for not returning your phone call about a job. I'm happy to see you've found a position."

She blushed scarlet, but nodded.

"Amber and I are leaving New York for a while." He put his hat on. "Best of luck to you, Madeline."

He took Amber's arm. "Let's go, darling."

As they walked away, Amber clutched Wellman's arm possessively, looked over her shoulder, smiled, and waved.

Outside, the wind blew, lifting Amber's hat. She caught it just before it became airborne. Her hair wasn't long enough to use a hat pin. They'd parked several blocks away. Tired of holding it on, she took it off and carried it with her share of the parcels. Wellman merely settled his on tighter and bent his head against the wind.

Wellman tossed their purchases in the back seat of the Packard and settled her in the passenger side. He slid behind the wheel, threw his arm over the back of the seat, and cleared his throat. Brow furrowed, he said, "I'm sorry, Amber, we can't afford to buy rings right now."

Oh dear. "Wellman, I wasn't implying I wanted a ring. My comment was a dig for Madeline's benefit." She flashed him an innocent smile. "You know, gloating, implying you were still financially secure." She sighed. "Actually, it was rather mean on my part. I feel a little ashamed."

He snorted. "For once she was on the receiving end. Don't worry about it." He started the car and pulled out into traffic. "Do you mind if we go by the bank? I need to tend to a few matters before we make travel arrangements."

"No, not at all."

As soon as he stopped in front of the bank, a doorman opened the door to help her out, and then ran around to the driver's side.

"Thanks, Steven. We'll be ready to leave in an hour so have the car back here by then." He started to walk off and then stopped. "By the way, this is my wife. She'll be coming in on occasion, so take good care of her."

The man grinned and doffed his hat. "Yes, sir. Nice to meet you, ma'am." Before she could respond, he'd slipped behind the wheel and was pulling away.

Inside was a large reception area big enough to accommodate the bank's lobby. Wellman escorted her to a corner office. When they entered, a young man sporting a blond mustache stood and circled the desk. "Good afternoon, Wellman." His pale gray eyes never left Amber and she squirmed under his scrutiny.

"Howard, this is my wife, Amber. Dear, this is my bank manager Howard Lancaster."

He took her hand. "Please to meet you, Mrs. Hathaway."

Amber exchanged a quick greeting and nodded.

"I need you to make sure she can draw money from my account and she's to have full access to the bank's books if she desires."

The man flushed. "Surely, Wellman, Mrs. Hathaway wouldn't understand the workings of a bank."

"I assure you, Mr. Lancaster, I'm quite qualified and well versed on the workings of the banking industry."

Wellman chuckled. "Howard, she's an investment banker."

The color in Howard's face deepened. He coughed and gasped for air. "I see. Very good, then."

Very good my ass, thought Amber. He doesn't want to share and sees me as a threat to his authority. Tough. She turned toward Wellman. "If it's okay, I'd like to go up to your office while you're busy."

"Of course, but first I'd like you to meet my secretary." Taking her arm, he ushered her across the hall from the lobby. As they passed she nodded to the smiling tellers. "I'll introduce you to them next visit. We're short on time today."

"Fine."

Wellman rapped on the door and entered before the occupant had a chance to say, "Come in." An attractive, stately woman in her forties rose from behind her desk as they entered. Smiling, she studied Amber carefully, but Amber saw no jealously in her appraisal, just curiosity. "Hello, Mr. Hathaway."

"Constance, I'd like for you to meet my wife. Amber, this is my well-trusted assistant, Constance Dyer." The smile on her face turned to shock but she quickly recovered and stepped forward.

"I'm so pleased to meet you, Mrs. Hathaway." Amber shook her outstretched hand.

"Thank you, Constance. Please call me Amber. I'll be working with you on occasion."

Constance, eyes wide and questioning, but too polite, or too well trained to be nosy, smiled and said, "I'd like that." She turned to Wellman. "Congratulations, sir."

"Thank you." Arm draped across Amber's shoulders, he led her to the door. "I'll be up shortly."

She left and walked down the hall toward the elevators. James, looking sharp in his navy and red wool uniform stood waiting for his next passenger, snapped to attention as she approached. "Fifth floor?" he asked.

"Yes, thank you."

"Miss Mathis isn't it?" he asked as she stepped inside.

When he closed the door, the four walls closed in on her and she panicked. Breath coming in gasps, she managed a weak laugh. "It's Mrs. Hathaway now."

"You don't say?"

"Yes, as of last night," said Amber. The elevator car lurched and, eyes closed, she pressed against the wall. What if when the door opened she was back in 2011? Did she want to go back?

"Mrs. Hathaway?" Her eyes popped open to see James waiting for her with the door open. "Fifth floor."

She pushed away from the wall. "Sorry. Daydreaming." Noting the accordion gate pushed to the side, she sighed with relief, stepped into the hallway, and proceeded to Wellman's office. Inside, she removed her coat and tossed it over the back of the sofa. At the tall window, she looked out on the 1930s street below and breathed a sigh of relief. No, she didn't want to find the way back, even if she could. Here, she had a much better purpose. With her knowledge, she could help Wellman and others find the way back to prosperity.

~*~

March 5, 1930, Amber and Wellman stopped at a florists shop close to Lutheran Hospital. Smells of fresh flowers filled her nostrils as they walked inside. Large vases sat on counters around the colorful room. Amber was immediately drawn to the display of white roses in crystal vases. "These, Wellman, a dozen of these will be perfect."

"Pick whatever you like," he said while looking at an exhibit of books.

While the clerk rang up their purchase, Wellman placed a box on the counter. "Here, let's get this too."

At the sight of his addition, her heart pounded. It was a Bible just like the one Gram had treasured so, the one she'd lovingly placed in her hands with a long stemmed white rose before the people from the funeral home closed her casket. For a minute she swayed on her feet and feared she'd faint.

Wellman caught her around the waist. "What's wrong? Do you need to sit down?"

She shook her head and whispered, "No, just…I'll tell you in a minute."

"Would you like for me to wrap this for you?" The clerk asked.

"Yes," said Wellman. "Please, something for a baby girl." He led her to a corner of the shop. Hands on her shoulders, he ordered, "Tell me."

"The Bible. It's just like the one I buried Gram with. She cherished it so. Though I wanted to keep it, I also wanted her to have it always." Her heart thumped at what was happening here. "Inside, she kept a dried flattened flower between a folded piece of wrapping paper.

"*This* paper," she murmured as the clerk walked forward with the box and placed it in her hands. Amber lovingly ran her hand over the crisp new paper decorated with pink baby booties. It was the same pattern, the design she'd seen for so many years as faded and yellow—and now here it was pristine and new. "I realize the flower inside the bible was a white rose bud." She reached out and touched a stem in the vase he held in the crook of his arm. "The petals of one of these."

Tears threatened. She choked back a laugh and said, "I know this doesn't make sense, but somehow all these coincidences make me feel better about being here in 1930. Like it was meant to be. No one in 2011 will miss me. The only relative I left behind is an elderly uncle who is too ill to know I'm gone."

She couldn't blame him for his dubious expression, but he smiled and said, "I'm glad, Amber." With his free arm, he opened the shop door. When they were outside, his hand palmed the base of her back as they walked the few blocks to Lutheran Hospital. She could feel its heat through the suit she wore—a sensation that warmed her in other places.

It didn't take them long to find Adam and Rosemary Goldstein and their new baby girl, Martha. They stood at the door and watched as her great-grandfather sat against the pillows beside her great-grandmother with their infant in her arms. Wellman rapped on the doorframe. "Hello, may we come in?"

Surprised, the couple looked up. "Do we know you?" her great-grandfather asked.

Wellman walked in and offered his hand. "No, I don't think so. I'm Wellman Hathaway and this is my wife, Amber."

Adam Goldstein stood and approached them. "I'm Adam Goldstein and this is my wife, Rosemary, and our daughter, Martha." He looked back and forth between them, his eyes lingering on Amber. "If we don't know you, why are you here?"

Amber couldn't believe these were actually her grandmother's folks. They'd died before she was born so she'd only seen the old photographs Gram had in the family album. She'd give anything to be able to throw her arms around them and hug them. They'd probably think she was nuts and call security.

"Actually," she said grabbing Wellman's arm and leaning into his side. "We're here because your baby girl has won the New Baby Contest for this week." She walked forward and handed the wrapped Bible to her great-grandmother. "This is for baby Martha."

"A contest?" asked Rosemary as she took the package. "We didn't enter a contest." She turned to her husband. "Did we, dear?"

Adam shook his head. "Not to my knowledge."

"Oh, I'm sorry, I should have explained," said Amber. "Your names came from the newspaper this morning. We put all the new babies in a drawing and baby Martha was the lucky winner."

"Well, I'll be," said Adam. He joined his wife and

watched as she ripped the paper from the box.

"A Bible! Oh, how special," gushed Rosemary. "Thank you. We'll cherish it always."

Wellman snatched a white rose bud from the bouquet and handed the vase to Adam. He broke the stem. "Eleven roses are for you, Mrs. Goldstein, but this bud is for Martha from her two new admirers." He laid it on top of the Bible.

Amber approached the bed and looked down at her grandmother's pink face, little rosebud mouth, and full head of dark hair. Is this what her child would look like if she ever had one? Her throat closed with emotion. "She is so beautiful." She bit her bottom lip to stifle the tears of joy that threatened. Voice hoarse, she croaked. "We better go." She patted Rosemary's knee. "You need your rest."

"But wait," said Rosemary. "Wouldn't you like to hold her?"

Emotion clogging her throat, she croaked out, "You wouldn't mind?"

"Of course not. We'd be honored."

Adam lifted the baby and placed her in Amber's arms. She thought her heart would literally burst with pleasure at the contact. Unable to resist, she laid her cheek against the baby's head. *I love you, Gram.*

~*~

Amber had looked so natural with the baby in her arms. Their coloring was so similar she could easily pass for Martha's mother. Now Amber smiled and had such a glow about her it brought a lump to Wellman's throat. She would probably be a wonderful mother. He wanted children…someday.

They'd not made love since that first time. In case

they did, he'd laid in a supply of condoms, but he avoided close contact as much as possible. It was killing him. She looked, smelled, and when they ventured to touch, felt like heaven. No, he didn't want to have children with this woman. He didn't want to fall in love with her. Not today or ever.

He watched as she carefully laid the infant back in its mother's arms and turned toward him. "I guess we better go and let you get some rest."

"Thank you so much for the gifts," said Mrs. Goldstein.

"Yes, thank you," said Adam. "It was a nice surprise. One we'll share with Martha when she's older."

Wellman took Amber's elbow and eased her back from the bed and said. "You've very welcome."

In the elevator, Amber fell back against the wall, joy on her face. "I actually held my grandmother in my arms." She laid her hand across her heart. "I'm going to be all right. Holding her, I felt something inside me shift, lift. Now I know, regardless of what happens in Kilgore, I'll be fine."

"Well, I'm pleased your mind is relieved," he muttered.

"I am. We'll both be rich. You'll be able to pay your depositors, divorce me, and can go on with your life. I'll get an apartment, a job," she shrugged, "if I want to work, and start a new life." She poked him in the arm. "Both our problems solved."

The elevator attendant shot her a shocked glance but averted his head at Wellman's glare.

Her reassurance should have soothed his worries, but in fact made him uncomfortable. He wasn't sure he wanted her to make it on her own. *Yes, you do. Don't let down your guard. She'll break your heart.*

~*~

What had she been thinking? The idea of traveling on a train, sleeping in a Pullman car had sounded exciting. Shoved up against the wall in the lower berth, listening to the snores, and smelling the body odors of her fellow travelers made her want to scream. On both sides, they were lined up in a row, five singles on the top, and five doubles on the bottom. All that provided privacy was a dividing curtain between each and one on the outside. Thank goodness the seat back offered them a little more privacy. Beside her, Wellman snored softly. She fumed. By God, if she was going to be miserable, she intended to have company.

With her pointer finger, she gigged him in the side.

He jumped. "What...was that for? Am I snoring too loud?" he murmured.

"No. I can't sleep with the racket in here." Leaning up on her elbow, she pounded her pillow and whispered through clenched teeth, "It stinks in here, it's loud, and this bed is too narrow. I'm so frustrated I'm ready to scream!"

As if on cue, a loud coughing echoed through the sleeping car. With a hiss, she drew in a lungful of air. In a flash, Wellman flattened her against the mattress, his hand covered her open mouth and all that escaped her lips was an "eek."

"Are you crazy?"

She sniggered against his hand.

"Shhh. You're...going to wake people." He rolled to his back taking her with him, her face smashed against his bare chest.

She felt the tremors shake his body and yanked his chest hair.

"Ouch!" he wheezed.

"You're laughing too."

He chuckled. "Yeah, well, it's your fault." He wrapped his arms around her. "Be still now and try to go to sleep."

"If we have a chance to get off the train tomorrow, I'm buying some ear plugs." And some deodorizer too. The car had a dressing room with one shower each for the women and one for the men. It was like being in college again sharing a community bathroom. Tomorrow morning she intended to be the first one in that single shower.

She yawned and listened to the steady thump of Wellman's heart, concentrating on its rhythm rather than the noises around her. His chest hair tickled her nose and she blew to displace it. Her hand smoothed over his muscled ribcage. What did he do to stay so fit?

Their first night of lovemaking hadn't been repeated. If their coming together hadn't been so passionate and satisfying, she'd think he didn't desire her. She knew that wasn't true. He wanted her, just as she did him. He didn't want to love her. They were agreed on that point. She didn't want to care for someone who had no desire to love her. It was best if they kept their relationship platonic.

The passenger car rocked gently as it sped down the track. Each mile took them closer to Texas and their oil fortune. *Lordy, she prayed her memory of the oil discovery was correct.* Her breathing slowed and she joined him in sleep.

On March twelfth, two days after leaving

Manhattan on the New York Central, they arrived in Chicago. After a short layover, they boarded the Midnight Special to St. Louis. Upon arrival, Amber had had her fill of traveling by rail but it would have taken too long to finish the journey by car. Tired and bedraggled, grumbling at Wellman's lack of ill temper, she allowed him to drag her aboard the Sunshine Special. Thirty-six hours later, on March fifteenth, they arrived in Kilgore, Texas.

Five

Amber had never seen so much rain in her life. Mud from the dirt streets sucked at their shoes as they slogged across the street from the station. A reed thin hotel clerk rushed forward, took their bags, and set them beside the check-in counter.

Amber and Wellman peeled off their wet, mud-coated footwear and set them on the piece of newspaper by the iron wood stove. Amber hovered near the heat trying to warm her toes.

Wellman asked, "How much for a room?"

"A dollar a day." The young clerk turned the register around for Wellman to sign in.

"We need something long term. Do you have a weekly rate?"

"Nope, I'm real sorry, only the daily fee." He scratched his chin. "I can put out word around town. With these hard times there might be someone wantin' to rent a room in their home."

The next day they settled into the spare room in the home of a Mrs. Danvers, a widow lady with a house a half mile outside of town. Rent of seventy-five cents a day included breakfast and dinner.

Drilling was taking place on several farms outside of town, but there had been no strikes. The wildcatters filled the bars at night. They drank all night, slept a couple of hours and then went back to work. No wonder accidents were a common occurrence on rigs. One slip with rigging and a man lost a hand or arm.

Since arriving in Kilgore in March, Wellman and Amber frequented the restaurants at noontime, the bars at night and listened to the talk about oil. If she heard the wildcatter's name that'd brought in the well after the Daisy Bradford #3 on October 3, 1930, Amber knew it would ring a bell.

The May breeze blew clean and fresh through the open window of Alva Danvers's Model A Ford Coupe, which she had kindly loaned them. Wellman drove slowly to reduce the amount of dust kicked up as the vehicle covered the short distance over the rutted dirt road that led to Fred's Roadhouse. Amber watched the fading light setting in the West. She didn't look forward to another night of crowd watching.

Inside the bar, they found a table near the dance floor. As she sat down, Amber smoothed the mid-calf skirt over her thighs. She'd wanted to wear her new wool slacks, but Wellman insisted she attire herself appropriately, in a dress. At lease her shoes had low heels and were comfortable.

Clean, his clothes neatly pressed, Wellman looked out of place amid the work soiled men. As usual, he received odd looks from some of the rowdy men, and Amber held her breath hoping there wouldn't be trouble. Wellman was muscled but she wasn't sure he'd be able to handle himself if these guys got disorderly and tried to pick a fight.

Music from a jukebox blared in the smoky room of Fred's Roadhouse. It smelled of unwashed bodies, fried food, and dime store perfume. Few men had wives with them but a number of single women frequented the bar in hopes of a few free beers and the opportunity to dance. And dance they did. Folks back in the thirties knew how to boogie. Amber tapped her foot to the music. She'd love to learn how to Jitterbug.

"You ready for something to eat?" Wellman stood. "I'm about to cave in."

"Sure. I'll have a hamburger. You need some help?"

"Nope, I can handle it. You stay here and save our table."

A good idea since every table in the place was taken. If she and Wellman didn't discover oil, maybe they could open a bar. Looked like the owners here were making a good living. They worked hard for every penny though. She'd hate to put up with this kind of crowd every night.

She felt a hand on her shoulder. "Hey, little lady. I see your pretty boyfriend is busy."

Amber looked up into the leering face of a dark-haired man. His beard was several days old and made him look like a swarthy pirate, albeit a handsome one. In his thirties, he wore his shirtsleeves rolled up to show bulging biceps. He loomed over her, leaning in close giving her an unwelcome whiff of stale sweat. Her stomach churned in rebellion and she shifted away to distance herself from him.

He took her hand and tugged. "Come dance with me, darlin'."

Amber yanked her hand from his. "I don't think so, but thanks for asking." She resisted the need to scrub her palm on her dress.

Hands the size of baseball mitts gripped her upper arms. He jerked her from the chair and held her flush with his body. Face just inches from his, she turned her head to avoid the heat and smell of his beer breath as he cooed, "Now, honey, that's no way to be friendly. I just want a little dance." His hand snaked around her waist and squeezed her hip.

Bile rose in her throat at his smell. Her skin crawled at his touch. A scream of panic clogged her throat. She fought to remain calm and swallowed her hysteria. She shoved against his chest, but he didn't budge. "Let me go," she hissed.

"Stuck up, bit—"

The man was yanked from behind and thrown onto the dance floor where he twirled, barely missing several dancers. Couples parted and moved out of the way.

Amber stared at the frozen features on her husband's face. A tic pulsed below his cheekbone and both hands were clenched as he fixed the pirate with his stare. "Don't ever put your hands on my wife again."

The drunken wildcatter jumped to his feet and grinned. "Think you can keep me from it, pretty boy?"

Wellman bit out, "I know I can."

The man hooted with laughter and started toward Wellman, fists raised.

Oh, God. Wellman wouldn't have a chance against the work hardened man. Sure, Wellman had nice muscles, but he worked behind a desk, not lifting heavy equipment every day. The other man was built like a tree, and though drunk, his stance was steady, the look in his eyes evil. She grabbed her husband's arm. "Come on, you don't have to do this. Let's go home."

Wellman didn't even look at her, kept his eyes on the pirate. "Get your hand off me and stay out of the way."

Well, hell. He was going to get hurt, bad.

"Better listen to the lady, man. I'd hate to mess up that pretty face of yours."

"Shut up and worry about your own ugly mug."

The drunk growled at the insult and charged. Before he got one swing in, Wellman hit him three times in the face. Women screamed. Blood spurted from his mouth and nose. The man went down like a felled tree. The fight was over in less than a minute.

People clapped and whistled. Amber could only gape. Her husband was a boxer. He moved like Rocky Balboa in the movie *Rocky.* That's how he kept that tall lanky body in such good shape. He worked out in the ring.

She felt faint with relief and hung on to a post to support herself. A gasp of pride escaped her lips and she smiled at the crowd's response. Excited voices flew around the room.

"Did you see that?"

"Man moved faster than lightening."

One man chuckled. "Bet that's the last time Jones messes with some man's wife."

The owner pushed through the crowd carrying a baseball bat. Almost seven feet tall, and wearing a large white apron, his face and stance brooked no argument. "We don't allow fighting in here, mister. I'll thank you to leave."

Wellman nodded, face red from embarrassment or anger, Amber didn't know which. He put his arms around her and held her close. "Are you all right?"

She answered against his starched shirt, thankful for the strength and safety he exuded. "I'm fine." His concern made her heart swell with a longing she didn't want to name.

He cupped her cheek and studied her eyes before taking her elbow, turning her toward the door.

"Now wait a minute, Fred," called an older man. Tall, with a bit of a paunch, he hitched up his pants as he walked. "This man was just protecting his wife. Jones tried to drag her out on the dance floor and she didn't want to go."

Fred arched a shaggy graying eyebrow. "Is that right, mister?"

"Yes." Wellman's answer was clipped and unapologetic.

The owner turned to Amber. "Are you all right, ma'am?"

"I'm fine. Thank you."

"Okay, your supper is on the house tonight." Fred hailed a waitress. "Bring this man a cold cloth and iodine for his hands." He turned to look at Jones sprawled on the dance floor, and then waved at a group of men standing around the unconscious drunk. "Get him out of here."

His cronies picked him up and moved toward the door.

Amber and Wellman sat down at their table. He turned to their rescuer. "Would you like to join us, have a bite to eat?"

He pulled out a chair and dropped into it. "I've already eaten but would be happy to sit and visit a spell."

The waitress appeared with first-aid supplies and their dinner. Amber cleaned Wellman's hands and spread the orange antiseptic all over his knuckles as their guest chatted. "Never seen anyone move that fast, son, outside of the boxing ring that is. You a professional?"

"Hardly," said Wellman. "I was on the boxing team in college." He flexed his hands and smiled at her. "Thank you, dear. Now, let's eat. I'm starved." He picked up his burger, but before taking a bite, turned to the older man. "You sure you won't have something to eat, Mr...?"

"I'm positive." He offered his hand. "Name's Tyner, Ted Tyner but folks around here call me Pop Tyner."

Wellman shook his hand. "It's good to meet you, Mr. Tyner. I'm Wellman Hathaway and this is my wife, Amber."

Wellman started eating, but Amber could only stare. This was the man. The one who they needed to find oil for them, the one who discovered the first wells a few blocks from downtown.

He nodded to Amber. "Ma'am. Where you folks from?"

"New York," she squeaked.

"Ooowee, you're a long way from home. Thought you were foreigners from your accent. What brings you to Kilgore?"

Heart racing, she said, "We came to find you."

"Me?" He looked at them in confusion. "What about?"

Wellman looked up from his burger and she mouthed *he's the one.* He laid his burger down and wiped his hands on his napkin.

"My wife and I have it on good authority that there's a lot of oil in this town and that you're the man who can find it."

~*~

Amber, hand over her mouth to stifle her giggles, bounced down the hall to their room. The minute the door was closed, she dove for the bed, and face buried in a pillow, which did little to muffle her squeals of, "We did it, we did it!"

Wellman grinned at her fervor hoping her excitement wouldn't be short lived. "We haven't struck oil yet, Amber. Don't get too excited."

She sat up. Her hair mussed, her cheeks rosy from excitement, she'd never looked lovelier. He ducked his head to hide the hunger he knew radiated in his eyes.

"But, we found the man, the one who discovered Lila Simpson's Number One, Number Two, and Number Three, the largest producing wells in town." Smoothing her skirt, she kicked off her shoes and bent to pick them up. He smiled at her exuberance and hoped it would be well served. "And, he said he'd drill for us. I can't believe he can get started with ten thousand dollars. It seems such a piddly amount."

"It may seem small from your perspective, but it's a big chunk of our mere forty-thousand." He'd yet to fully comprehend the difference in the cost-of-living in her time period. The fact that a dollar could buy so little appalled him.

"Yeah, I know. You're right." She grabbed the flannel shirt she slept in and her robe and trotted out the door for the bathroom.

"Don't take all night in there—"

The door closed, cutting him off. Wellman was glad to see her so animated. And thank God they wouldn't have to hang around the bar any longer. He didn't like her being exposed to the rowdy crowd hanging out there. When he'd seen that man's hand on her hip, he'd wanted to kill. How dare that man touch Amber with such familiarity? She was his wife, by God. He clenched his fists, wincing at the pain.

He'd removed his shirt, boots, and socks when Amber waltzed in wearing the shirt that hung on her frame and hit her just above the knees. Her robe was folded across her arm. After the first night or two, she'd chosen that over Madeline's cast off silk lingerie and he had to admit, her choice of sleepwear was sexy, tempting his imagination with what lay underneath. For several weeks now he'd fantasized about unbuttoning the soft shirt and easing it off her shoulders to taste her ivory skin.

She tossed her robe on the foot of the bed. "The bathroom is all yours." As he left the room, she sat on the bed rubbing lotion on her legs. The light floral scent was just one more thing to taunt him. He was beginning to think she did it on purpose. Why the hell he resisted her, he didn't know. Yes, he did. He was afraid he'd fall in love with her and he didn't intend to suffer that affliction again. Though he liked and admired her, she wasn't the type of wife he needed.

When he returned, she was bent over struggling to get lotion on her back. He sat down behind her on the bed and took the bottle. "Here, let me get your back for you."

"Oh, would you? I never can reach everywhere." She lifted her shirt to her shoulders baring her back to his gaze. Her white panties cupped her buttocks. He almost groaned out loud at the temptation they presented. His mind remembered how the globes fit his hand perfectly.

"Happy to help." Yeah, he loved to torture himself. He poured the cream in his hand and rubbed them together before smoothing it on over her shoulders. He'd gotten too much so it took a lot of stroking. In an effort to massage it in, he caressed her shoulders and down her sides. His mind on her derriere, with each pass he got closer. Her breathing hitched and he knew she was anticipating his moves. Did she want him to dip below the fabric and touch the soft mounds of her ass? At the hitch in her breath, he grinned. Yeah, she did.

Amber held her breath. Craving this man's touch, she reached back and drew the shirt over her head. "My arms could use some lotion, too." She wanted him to touch every inch of her, touch her and fan the flames that threatened to ignite inside her.

Voice gruff, he placed his lips against her shoulder and massaged lotion into her biceps, down over her forearms to her hands. "It's not your arms I'm interested in."

Heat shot through her body. She gulped to fill her lungs with air. "I know." She quickly removed her panties and stretched out on the bed on her stomach. "They're awfully dry and could use some moisture."

He shook the bottle and cold lotion plopped out on her ass. "Eek! That's cold."

His hand cupped a buttock and then moved to smooth the cream over her derriere. "I'll warm you." He straddled her hips and kneaded her eager, sensitized skin. "Do you know how lovely you are, Amber?"

She groaned, "No."

"You have the skin of a goddess."

She was drowning in the sensations his hands

evoked. His attention was now on her thighs, his thumbs moving nearer to her sex with each pass. *Oh, just a little closer,* her body cried. He stopped and moved off the bed.

No! Wait!

His pajama bottoms landed on top of her shirt. The bed sagged as he placed a knee on the bed. His large hands circled her waist, and before she could react, he flipped her onto her back. With a knee beside each of her thighs he studied her from her breasts to the juncture of her legs, his hands stroking the path his eyes touched. "Beautiful." He leaned down and covered one nipple with his lips, sucking gently. Unable to remain still, she squirmed beneath him and tugged his head trying to pull his lips to hers. She wanted his lips on hers, to taste him, to feel his breath mingle with hers. "Delicious." He evaded her grasp and turned to her other breast, laving it with his tongue. Jolts of yearning shot to her womb.

She reached around his waist and tried to pull him toward her, but he wouldn't budge. She wanted him now. A grin of mischievousness lit his smoky eyes. He sat back on his haunches and with his finger, traced circles around her puckered nipples, down around her navel then delving into the curls covering her sex. Wanting more of his touch, she arched toward his hand.

"Tell me you want me, Amber."

Gasping for breath, she moaned, "You know I do."

He trailed his lips across her collarbone, up to nuzzle her ear. "Tell me, darling."

"I want you, Wellman."

Lips on her neck, he opened her legs with one of his. His big hands clasped her buttocks and raised her to meet his thrust. She gasped as he entered her, her flesh welcoming his as he plunged and withdrew drawing wails of pleasure from deep in her throat. He drove her higher, the pleasure so intense she thought she'd scream. Suddenly, she shattered inside, her muscles clenching, thighs shaking from the force of her release. He dropped his head to her shoulder and joined her in climax.

Their bodies still connected, she stroked Wellman's back and floated on the rippling aftershocks of her orgasm. Never had she experienced such pleasure during sex. Her experiences, had been good, but sex with Wellman was beyond good, it touched her soul.

Head on his chest, Amber listened to Wellman's steady breathing as he slept. After their lovemaking, he cuddled her close but didn't speak. She wanted to talk, express how wonderful he made her feel, but didn't dare. Their lack of communication felt like a breach between them. His feelings were evident. He regretted their having sex. He didn't want to need her, desire her. Well, she didn't want to need him either.

~*~

Freshly shaven and smelling of Old Spice, Pop Tyner picked them up at seven o'clock the next morning in his Model T Ford Pickup. Squeezed between the two men, Amber watched in fascination as he shifted gears using different foot pedals. She'd expected to see the shift in the floorboard, but guessed that came with a later model.

Over breakfast at the local café, the older man discussed their choices as to drilling sites. After their dishes were cleared away, he spread a map of the area on the table and pointed out each one. Wellman glanced at Amber to see if any rang a bell. She shook her head.

"Which one would you pick?" asked Wellman.

Pop scratched his chin as he pondered the map. He took a pencil and drew Xs on three different spots, all in the downtown area. "These three are the ones I'm itching to break ground on. As to which one to start with, it's a toss of the coin."

Wellman looked at Amber. "Which one do you think?"

"I don't have a clue." She chewed her lip, her brow knitted in concentration. Cheeks pink with excitement, eyes alight with intelligence, he felt a twist of remorse in his gut. For the fiftieth time since their lovemaking last night, he wanted to kick himself. Touching her wasn't a good idea. It would be too easy to need her. He didn't want to need anyone, especially a woman who could destroy his heart again.

With her pointer finger, she traversed the map between the Xs. Finally, she stopped and tapped on the one two blocks off Main Street. "This one. Let's give it a try."

By noon, the widow lady, Mrs. Lila Simpson, who owned the property had signed a lease giving them permission to drill on all three lots. Pop Tyner assembled his crew. Late that afternoon, flatbeds began arriving on the drilling site with loads of lumber, tools, and drill stems and bits. Within a week, the beautiful bluebonnet filled plot became a dirty, rutted field. Outside their work area, the wildflowers gradually died and went to seed but now red Indian blankets grew amid pink primroses, and yellow ragweed.

Except for brief visits, Amber was banned from the

drill site. The woman was a ball of energy and if he'd let her, she'd pick up a hammer and start pounding nails. Wellman didn't want her around the roughnecks and their dirty mouths. She'd argued and insisted he'd be shocked to hear some of the language on television and in the movies in the future, but humored him and stayed out of the way. Drilling was dangerous work and he didn't need to worry about her when his mind should be on work.

By June they'd opened a small office for her on Main Street. From there Amber kept the books, paid the rowdies, and kept a list of men wanting work. It wasn't uncommon for someone to come in wanting to invest in their operation. Some big oil companies started sniffing around and tried to buy them out, but Wellman refused their offers.

During lulls at the office Amber made a list of possible future investments for them. Companies she knew would do well during the Depression and on into the war years. The war years. Wellman didn't like the idea their country would be embroiled in such a tragedy. The Pullman Company was on her list saying it would thrive into the sixties. He wasn't surprised there. If there was money to be made, Amber intended they be on the receiving end. She added companies he'd never heard of—DuPont, and some cosmetic companies. Without a doubt, women did love their makeup and perfumes.

~*~

By September, Amber was going stir crazy. Her office job didn't keep her fully occupied. Wellman came home from work totally exhausted. At night he did well to stay awake long enough to take a bath and eat. He fell into bed and was asleep the minute his head hit the pillow.

Amber knew the work was grueling. Wellman's toned body was now rock hard from lifting and turning those huge wrenches, not to mention the other pieces of equipment they manually carried from trucks to the rig itself. She didn't fail to notice the look of concern on his face each evening when he came in. They were already at 2800 feet without a sign of oil.

On the first evening in October when their landlady, Alva, came in from work at the cotton gin, Amber had dinner cooked and ready to put on the table. She chuckled at her sheer desperation for something to do. Next thing she'd be doing laundry. *Heaven forbid!* Not that she minded washing clothes, but the old wringer washer kept on the back porch wasn't what she was used to. At least Alva had an electric iron, a Sunbeam. They were lucky to be this close to town and have electricity. Many of the outlying farms were still using oil lamps. As far as laundry went, they'd just have to continue taking theirs downtown.

Alva came in through the back door. Her floral dress wrinkled from the day's heat, her ankles swollen above the lace up white shoes, the older woman's face was weary with exhaustion. "Are you having company, dear?"

"No. This is for us. I don't have enough to do so thought I'd start cooking the evening meal. I hope that's okay." Amber knew how tiring Alva's job was, yet each night she prepared a simple supper. Hopefully this would help. Tonight Amber had splurged and bought a small roast. She'd cooked carrots, potatoes, and green beans from the garden.

Mrs. Danvers paled. "That's very thoughtful, but I can't afford food like this."

"Oh, no, tonight's our treat. From now on, we can share grocery costs." She shrugged and grinned. "I can't cook a whole lot and am hoping in exchange you can teach me a few things."

"Well, I see your point." Mrs. Danvers relaxed slightly but frowned. "I suppose I should lower your rent."

"No, that's not necessary. Your rent is more than generous as it is. With more oil people coming in we may need to pay you more." Amber knew that in a short time people would be pitching tents to live in. She and Wellman were lucky to have arrived when they did. "Besides, you are generously letting us use your late husband's car."

"Well, I never learned to drive it and no one had any money to buy it from me." Then her lips thinned. "I hope you kids didn't put all your money into that well." She shook her head. "I don't have much faith in this getting rich quick oil dream."

Amber hoped she had her facts right and that they were drilling in an area that was part of the Woodbine Formation. But Alva didn't know Amber's prior knowledge and if she told her, the woman would think she was nuts.

"You go on and get comfortable. I'll have the table set when you get back."

The older woman's brow furrowed. "Well, if you're sure."

"I'm sure." Actually, she wasn't as confident as she sounded as their money was thinning daily, but they had to eat and one more mouth to feed wouldn't clean out their stash. There was no need to add worry to the woman's shoulders.

Amber heard thumping on the back porch and saw Wellman sitting on the stoop shaking his boots, his hat beside him. His damp hair held the crease of the hatband. She stood at the screen door and watched as he used his pocketknife to scrape away mud and dirt. "Hi. You're home early this evening."

He glanced up and a smile eased his tired features. "Yeah, we quit before time and left a few men on watch."

She went out and sat down beside him. "What's going on? You haven't given up, have you?"

He shook his head. She ran her hand through the wet stands of his blond hair. It had been over a month since he'd had a haircut. She reminded herself to make sure he got one tonight. Alva had a pair of hand clippers. Last time Amber cut his hair, she'd made quite a mess. She couldn't resist releasing a little snicker. Mrs. Danvers had to repair the damage she'd caused, but hopefully she'd do better this time.

"What are you laughing about?"

"Uh, you need a haircut."

He pulled back. "You're not touching my hair again. I'll pay the twenty cents for a professional cut in town."

Hand over her heart, she said, "I'm wounded. With a little practice, I'll be as good as Mrs. Danvers."

He snorted. "Feel free to find another poor soul to work on." Laughing, he rose and helped her up, held the screen door, and followed her inside in his sock feet.

Amber kept dinner warm until Wellman finished

his bath. She looked forward to sitting down to dinner with him—one where he was awake enough to talk. Alva puttered around the kitchen table, moving things so Wellman could reach the salt, pepper, and butter from where he sat. In this generation the man of the house was catered to, more so than in modern time.

Wellman entered looking too handsome for his own good and leaving a waft of his expensive aftershave in his wake. Mrs. Danvers removed her apron and placed it on the counter. "Mr. Hathaway, it's a pleasure to have you here at supper time for a change. You and those men work too long hours."

"That oil won't get out of the ground with us sitting at home." He held Amber's chair and rushed around to help seat Alva. "And when are you going to start calling me Wellman? I keep thinking you're talking to my father."

She waved him away. "I can sit myself. You just don't look like a Wellman to me, so you'll just have to put up with the Mr. Hathaway."

Wellman sighed and sat down. "Mmmm, this looks wonderful. You outdid yourself tonight, Alva."

She handed him the plate with the pot roast, potatoes, and carrots. "Amber cooked this meal."

Wellman looked up from the food in surprise.

"I got bored," said Amber. "Thought I'd help Alva out and start cooking dinner. I picked up groceries on my way home from the office."

"I didn't know you could cook."

"I'm not a gourmet chef but I can throw together a few good meals."

They ate in silence for a few minutes. The clatter of silverware against plates, ice in the glasses, and the buzz of cicadas in the backyard the only sounds to break the quiet.

Wellman laid his fork down and wiped his napkin across his mouth. "I've got some exciting news. They expect the Daisy Bradford #3 to blow on the third of this month."

"You don't say." Alva shook her head. "I'll believe it when I see it. I'm sorry to say it but I'm afraid you folks are just wasting your money and time reaching for a pipe dream."

Amber turned to Wellman. "How can they know that?"

"The samples they took a month ago showed oil and each sample since then has gotten richer. It'll be any day now or so says Dad Joiner." This was the third well Dad Joiner had drilled on the Bradford farm. The other two were spuds. She'd learned a lot of drilling terminology in the past few months. Spud meant a dry well.

"People from all around are going to come watch the well blow. There will be hamburger and lemonade stands. A barnstormer out of Dallas is giving airplane rides for two dollars."

A two-dollar airplane ride? What a concept.

Six

On Friday, they packed a picnic lunch and rode in Alva's car to the Bradford farm about nine miles southwest of Kilgore. They arrived at ten o'clock. Cars lined the pasture and they had to walk almost half a mile to the site. Before they left the house, Alva plopped a big floppy hat on Amber's head. She was grateful for the shade as they walked up the rutted path.

Amber had never seen anything like it before. People had made their own shade with tarps held up by poles. Every shade tree was occupied. She feared they'd be stuck in the hot sun all day and look like boiled lobsters by bedtime. It'd be nice to have a little twenty-first century sunscreen.

They'd about given up on finding a place when Pop Tyner climbed from under his tarp, hollered and waved them over. "Howdy, folks, come join us. We've got plenty of room."

Thank goodness. Amber stepped under the covering and dropped to the blanket. Alva sat down beside her. "Amber, this is Sarah Tyner, Pop's wife," said Wellman.

"I'm pleased to meet you, Mrs. Tyner." Amber offered her hand to the older woman. She took it in one hand and with the other patted it.

"You'll be calling me Sarah, Amber. I won't have it any other way," said Sarah. She turned to Alva. "It's good to see you. I'm sure glad to see the Hathaways are bunking at your place. You'll take good care of them."

Alva beamed at her friend. "It's been a blessing having the extra money. And to top it all, Amber has started cooking the evening meal."

Sarah turned toward Amber. "Is that a fact?"

"Yes, I'm getting bored with not enough to do at the office. I'm used to working ten to twelve hour days so I don't know what to do with my free time."

"I expect not having your own house to tend to leaves a gap in your day," said Sarah. "Lord knows, I work from sunup to sunset and never get everything done."

Amber didn't think she needed a house that took that much time. Of course, the two older women didn't have the convenience of modern science. Hopefully, she and Wellman would make enough money on oil for her to live comfortably. She'd prefer to work in an office rather than keep a house clean without twenty-first century appliances. When she and Wellman got their divorce, she'd buy an apartment in Manhattan. She glanced at her husband. A pang stung her heart.

Sarah's question interrupted her train of thought. "What type of job did you have in New York to work such hours?"

"I worked in banking. I'm an investment banker."

"Gracious," said Sarah. "I've never heard of a woman having that type of job."

"It's becoming more common every day. Women are becoming lawyers, doctors, and even politicians."

Sarah "tisk, tisked," and shook her head. "It ain't natural for a woman to be doing a man's job."

The men had been discussing drilling, but at

Sarah's "gracious," tuned into their conversation.

Pop added his two cents. "Now, Sarie, people up in the big city are different from us country folks." He turned to Alva. "You've never said anything about Alva working at the gin."

Alva straightened and looked at Sarah. Great, thought Amber. I hope this doesn't hurt Alva's feelings.

Sarah worried her bottom lip with her teeth, and patted her friend's hand. "But that's different. Alva didn't have a choice after her dear George died so sudden."

"That's right," said Pop. "And think about the number of women who've been forced to go to work to feed their kids since the stock market crash. Poor things, with jobs so scarce they're lucky to find even the most menial work."

"I 'spect you're right." She nodded to Amber. "I meant no offense. Guess some of my opinions are outdated."

"No matter," said Amber. "You have a right to express your opinion. And many people feel the way you do."

Wellman reached for their picnic basket. "We need to switch topics of conversation or before you know it we'll be discussing politics and religion." He started laying out food.

Pop hooted and slapped his leg. "Those are two areas us Texans have strong feelins' on. We don't need a heated debate on this fun day."

~*~

Wellman watched Amber eye the barnstormer and his passengers. She grinned as each rider got off, legs wobbly as they laughed and staggered into the arms of a parent, spouse, or friend.

"Why don't you take a ride?"

Her eyes widened. "We don't need to spend money on something so frivolous."

"We can afford two dollars for a plane ride. After all, when we get home, you may go back to the future." A stab of regret hit him in the chest at the possibility. He'd miss her but it would be for the best. They weren't suited for a life together. She'd even said he was stodgy and dull. Life with him would be boring, and she wasn't the type woman who'd be satisfied staying home to raise kids and cater charity functions. No, she was a career woman. They were worlds apart.

"I've flown in plenty of airplanes." She leaned closer. She smelled of lilac talcum powder. He resisted the urge to inhale deeply and savor the sweet scent he'd come to identify with her. "But the ones we have hold hundreds of people and the cabins are under pressure so you don't hear all that noise."

The Boeing Model 80, currently the most up-to-date passenger airliner, with a total seating capacity of seventeen, couldn't compete with that. He shook his head in amazement. "I can't imagine such a thing."

"You wouldn't believe how far the flight industry has come." Wide-eyed, she looked toward the small plane as it flew down the makeshift runway and lifted into the air.

Her experiences couldn't be anything like flying in a little open plane like the one that had just taken off. If the future has pressurized cabins, she needed to feel the wind take her breath away and lift her hair into the air. It was an experience one never forgot and he'd like her to take that memory back to the future with her. Maybe she'd remember and think of him. He stood, took her hand and pulled her up to stand in front of him. "Let's go get you in line."

"Don't you want to go for a ride?"

"I've been up several times."

A grin stretched her face. "Okay, if you're sure we can spare the money."

When the plane made its first roll, Amber almost peed her pants. She screamed and covered her eyes, shrieking, "Oh, shit, oh shit, oh shit!" when they stormed Mrs. Bradford's barn. The pilot buzzed the crowd bringing cheers from the throng. She thought her ten minutes would never end. At last, he flew over the trees and set down in the clearing close to where he'd lifted off. The plane rolled to a stop not far from people waiting in line.

Wellman jogged up to help her down from the craft. She fell into his arms, her knees wobbly. He wrapped an arm around her waist to keep her from falling. Laughing, he hugged her against his side. "Well, what did you think?"

She snorted. "I'll never go up again. Couldn't you hear me screaming over the noise of the motor?"

"Yep, I could." He chuckled. "But I was trying to be a gentleman and not mention the fact."

"I hope the pilot couldn't hear my cursing." She looked around. "Where's the bathroom? I'm about to wet my pants."

"That bad, huh?" He steered her in the direction of the trees. Outhouses had been set up for the occasion. Not thrilled at the idea of using one, she bit back her distaste and hurried to take care of business. It was stifling inside, but being new, relatively clean.

Outside, she breathed in the fresh air. Why couldn't it be cooler? She almost wished it would rain.

By seven o'clock, people had given up on witnessing a gusher. They packed up and gradually, the hundreds of vehicles drove away. Fear closed around Amber's heart, squeezing so hard she feared she might be having a heart attack. The expression on Wellman and Pop's faces didn't ease her discomfort. Worry etched Wellman's brow and Pop wouldn't look at her. If someone didn't find oil soon, they were in a heap of trouble.

~*~

Pounding on the front door woke Wellman from a deep sleep. Hell, it wasn't even dawn and he'd tossed and turned all night and fallen asleep an hour ago. The noise sounded again. He bounded from the bed and stepped into his work pants and then his shoes. Damnation! He hoped there wasn't trouble at the rig.

Amber mumbled, "What's wrong?"

"Don't know. Go back to sleep. I'll see who it is. Probably someone from the site needing something."

"'Kay." She turned over and was asleep before he left the room. He opened the door to find Pop on the front porch.

Hair a mess like he'd just climbed from bed, a grin stretched the old man's face. "The Daisy Bradford blew last night."

Wellman couldn't contain the yell that rushed from his mouth. Sleeping birds flew from the tree in the front yard.

Pop had held his excitement in as long as he could. He released a loud, "Yee ha!" and grabbed Wellman in a bear hug. "We're gonna be rich, son. I know it."

The front door opened and Amber stepped out, Alva on her heels. Both women had hastily thrown on robes. Alva demanded. "What is going on out here? You're going to wake the entire county."

Pop released him and Wellman grabbed Amber by the waist and swung her around in the air. He'd been so worried that Amber had made a mistake and that there was no oil in the area. Now they had proof—it was here—somewhere.

He set her on her feet. "The Daisy Bradford blew last night."

Her face lit up like a neon sign. She threw her arms around his neck and squealed with joy in his ear. He caught her close and whispered, "Now, don't get your hopes up too high. This is just a good sign. That's all."

She kissed his neck. "I know. I'll try to remain objective."

Pop couldn't restrain his excitement. He chattered a mile a minute. "We're next, boys and girls. I just know we're next."

Alva slapped him on the arm. "Now, don't be getting your hopes up, old man. Just because there is oil out on Daisy's farm, doesn't mean it's in Kilgore." She looked from Pop to them. "Though I do declare, I never dreamed in a million years that well would come in."

She turned and started for the door. "Y'all might as well come on in and let me fix you some breakfast. I doubt anyone will be able to sleep now."

~*~

A month later, tests results came back on the Lila Simpson. There was little doubt oil was in the ground where they were drilling. Just when they'd reach it, no one knew. Pop and Wellman rotated shifts so that one of them was at the site at all times. A week later, one of the crew came in the middle of the night for Wellman. A gang of ruffians had destroyed their derrick, and Pop was in the hospital. They'd used an ax handle and broken his leg. He also had a slight concussion. The rest of the crew were battered and bruised but could work.

Amber and Wellman visited him in the hospital.

"Who did this, Pop?" Wellman's face resembled a piece of granite. A muscle ticked in his jaw. Amber had never seen him so angry.

"That piece of trash, Jones, and his cronies."

"But, why?" asked Amber.

"Because he's a worthless piece of cow dung," said Pop. "He got fired from the Daisy Bradford crew for drinking on the job."

"I expect," said Wellman, "he still holds a grudge against me because I bloodied his nose." He patted Pop's good leg. "Don't you worry, I'll take care of this. We'll have the derrick back up by tomorrow and be back to drilling."

"I'm mighty sorry, son. It's gonna be a big expense."

He looked at Amber. "We've got a little money left. We're too close not to continue. You get well and come back to work when you can."

Amber had to run to keep up with him as they left the hospital. "Where are we going?"

"You're going to the office."

"No, I'm going with you."

"Suit yourself, but stay out of my way. It's not going to be pretty."

They'd borrowed Alva's car and the tires threw gravel as Wellman peeled out of the parking lot. Ten minutes later they pulled in the rutted yard in front of Fred's Roadhouse. Though it was just after noon, several cars were parked at odd angles and music from the jukebox blared.

It was dark inside, but light enough to see Jones at the bar entertaining the waitress on duty.

Wellman stopped just inside the door and put his hand on her arm. "You are not to come any farther. Do you understand me?" He caught her chin in a big hand. "And do not interfere. I mean it, Amber."

She could only nod as the knot of fear in her stomach curled tighter.

He strode toward the bar and stopped ten feet from Jones. The waitress saw him and must have recognized the rage on his face as she scurried to get back to work and out of the way. Jones pushed himself away from the bar. "Well, lookie here. If it ain't pretty boy? Heard you had some trouble over to the Lila Simpson last night."

"I'm sure you did since you were there swinging an ax handle. First it was manhandling women, now you're beating up old men. What's next, you piece of scum? Children?"

Jones guffawed. "You got no proof that was me."

"Oh but I do. Pop identified you."

He snickered. "Just his word against mine."

"I beg to differ." Wellman reached in his pocket and withdrew a scrap of cloth. "I believe this will match the tear in your shirt perfectly."

Jones looked down at the gaping hole where his pocket had been. A dingy undershirt shone through. He snarled. "Well, what are you gonna do about it, pretty boy?"

Fred appeared at the bar, bat in hat. "You'll take it outside or I'll be crackin' both your heads."

"Fine by me," said Wellman. He waved toward Jones. "After you."

Jones hoisted his pants up and started for the door. "You took me by surprise last time, but today I'm going to beat you to a bloody pulp, Hathaway."

Amber moved out of the way as they passed and then pressed up against the outer wall. She wanted to slide to the ground in a heap, but instead looked around for something she could use for a weapon in case Wellman needed help. Every customer in the building filed out to watch the show, Fred included, still carrying his bat. She moved to Fred's side and reached for the shaped piece of ash.

He held it away from her reach and grinned down at her. "He won't need your help, young lady. Your husband can take care of himself."

Amber turned her eyes toward Wellman and Jones. Fred's words reassured her but she'd still have felt better with the bat in her hand. The two men circled each other. Head down, Jones charged and caught Wellman in the abdomen knocking him to the ground. As Wellman rolled to stand up, Jones caught him in the ribs and back with his booted feet. Wellman yelled in pain and Amber stifled a scream.

Amber doubted Wellman had never been in a street fight. But, he caught on fast. He grabbed Jones's foot and twisted sending the man face down in the dirt. By the time he recovered his feet, Wellman was up and delivering punches to his face. When Jones went down, Wellman yanked him up and holding him by the shirt front continued to pummel his face.

If he didn't stop, he'd kill the man. "Wellman," she screamed and ran to him. "That's enough." She grabbed his arm and pulled. He let Jones fall to the ground in a heap.

A car roared into the yard and came to a screeching halt. People scattered to get out of its way. A barrel of a man, star pinned to his chest, got out carrying a shotgun. "What the hell is going on here?"

Wellman was winded and sucking in air. Fred spoke up. He waved at Wellman. "This fella claims Jones is the one that beat up Pop Tyner last night and destroyed his derrick, Sheriff."

He turned to Wellman. "Is that a fact?"

Wellman could only nod.

The sheriff scratched his chin. "Got any proof he was the one? Heard Pop had identified him but it'd be nice to have some evidence."

Amber pulled the torn shirt material from Wellman's pocket and handed it to him.

"Well, well, Jones. Looks like you just bought yourself a one way ticket out of town." He returned his shotgun to his car and came back to Jones, flipped him over like a sack of potatoes, cuffed his hands, and then pulled him to his feet. As he hustled the man to his car, he stopped by Wellman. "Tell Pop I'm right sorry and that this piece of trash will be in the next county by nightfall." He scorched the group hanging around with his gaze. "Most of you folks know the rules around here, but just in case I'm repeatin' 'em. When you're given a ticket out of this county, it means don't come back. If I see you, I shoot first and then ask questions." Heads bobbed up and down.

Seven

The repairs to their derrick took the rest of their money. Amber looked for a part time job to pay their living expenses. Her prospects weren't good as there just weren't jobs available. Wellman wired his father. The older man sold several pieces of art and sent them enough to live on for another month.

It was the second week of November and the weather had turned crisp. Amber closed the office at noon to walk home for a bite of lunch. She buttoned her coat up to her neck to keep out the cold air. She was almost at the house when the ground shook and she heard a loud roar. *What on earth?* Oh, God, something had exploded. Or was it an oil fire?

She turned back to town. The sky above was black near the railroad tracks where oil spewed from the ground and shot up into the sky. The Lila Simpson had blown. She took off at a run, exhilaration pumping through her veins. The wedge heeled shoes wobbled on the dirt road but did little to slow her progress. By the time she reached the rig, every man was busy working to cap the well and contain the oil. Manning the large wrenches, muscles bunched in effort, their lips were drawn back to show broad smiles on their greasy faces. A crowd of supporters had gathered. Their cheers competed with the roar from the well. Amber stood with them, watching, letting the spray of black crude rain down on her. It'd be hard to get clean but she didn't care. An hour later, the well was contained. Then the men went crazy yelling, hugging, and slapping each other on the back.

Wellman looked up and saw her. His grin widened, highlighting his white teeth in his oil covered face. She ran to meet him. He caught her under the arms and swung her around and around in the air. If he let go she'd sail a mile away.

She wrapped both arms around his neck and squealed. "Put me down! I'm getting dizzy."

He sat her on her feet, held her tight, and whispered in her ear. "We did it, sweetheart. We really did it!"

God, she hoped they had. She prayed the well would produce as they needed it to. Only then would they know for sure.

~*~

The Lila Simpson was producing twenty thousand barrels of oil a day. Wellman and Pop started construction on derricks on Mrs. Simpson's other two lots. On December 15, 1930, the Lila Simpson Number Two blew in producing eighteen thousand barrels a day. They were rich, well, maybe not yet but they were on their way. Amber started sending Howard Lancaster, Wellman's bank manager, money to make monthly payments to the bank's depositors. Oil was selling for one dollar and ten cents a barrel. If the wells continued at the rate they were going, they could send a check to Mr. Hathaway reimbursing him fully for funding their venture and be in the green by February or March 1931.

Oil workers from across the country filed into Kilgore looking for work. Wellman sent a man or two to the office almost every day to be added to the payroll. On December 28, 1930 the J.K. Lathrop in nearby Gregg County came in producing twenty-two thousand barrels a day. Then on January 26, 1931, the Lathrop No. 1 near Longview blew in at twenty thousand barrels a day. It soon became evident that the wells were all connected—below the ground lay a giant black ocean encompassing over one hundred forty thousand acres.

Overnight word of the strike spread and the next morning, citizens of Kilgore woke to find families camping on their lawns, in their pastures, and in churches. The town grew from seven hundred to ten thousand in the space of a few days. Prices on everything went up, everything except oil. At one point it sold for a dime a barrel, whereas a gallon of water cost a dollar. Oil derricks went up all over town. Buildings were leveled to make room.

Wellman insisted, after expenses, Amber set aside half of their profit for herself. Her little nest egg was growing rapidly. The fact gave her little pleasure, as money wasn't the important issue in her life at the moment. Nothing had changed between them. They enjoyed each other's company, but no words of commitment had been exchanged. Oh, she knew Wellman cared for her, but he'd not said, "I've changed my mind. I love you. Stay with me and be my wife."

To make matters worse, she was in love with him. If she told him her feelings, maybe he'd… Hell, she was grasping here. It wouldn't change things. Without him in her life, she might as well return to her own time—if such a thing were possible and she was certain it was not, but she could be as miserable there as she would be here. In the future, she'd know he was beyond her reach. In time, she might be able to get over him, move on. The idea became a nagging suggestion at the back of her mind.

One afternoon, Wellman and Pop entered the oil office. Wellman poured himself a cup of coffee from the pot on the wood stove that kept the room warm. From the frown he wore, something was wrong. Before she could ask, Pop spoke up and ended her curiosity.

"The sheriff shot that no account Jones this morning."

Amber blurted. "What for?"

Pop lifted his shoulders. "Sheriff told him not to step foot back in the county and Jones didn't listen. Not one to have to tell folks something twice, Sheriff shot him."

"Is he dead?"

"Naw, just wounded him in the shoulder. He'll get good treatment in the county jail."

"Why didn't he just arrest him, why shoot him?"

"Folks around here know what get out of town means—don't come back or face a bullet."

By August of 1931, the National economy couldn't support the flow of oil coming from "The World's Richest Acres." A cap was placed on the amount of oil pumped each day. The Governor of Texas called in the Texas National Guard to enforce it. Wellman and Pop, along with every oil man in the area, were furious their oil output was limited. The criminal activity grew worse in the burgeoning town. Drillers fought against the restriction, some resorting to any available means to deceive those in charge. The once quiet town became a haven for every form of riff raff. Crime rose. So much so, the Texas Rangers, led by "Lone Wolf" Gonzaullas, were called in to establish order. At one point, he made one hundred arrests a day and hooked his prisoners together with a heavy chain. Kilgore had begun work on a jail, but it wasn't finished so Gonzaullas marched them into the Baptist Church.

Wellman wanted Amber to return to New York where it was safer. He'd hired a man to work in the office with her, one big enough to protect her if necessary. She agreed to the bodyguard to pacify her husband and hoped the discussion was over. If she left, she feared things would be over between her and Wellman. She wasn't ready for that.

~*~

Wellman looked down at his filthy clothes. With his hat, he beat at his pants in an effort to remove some of the dust. Never in his wildest flights of fancy had he imagined he'd enjoy working at manual labor like he was now, but he did. It was satisfying to go home physically tired at the end of the day. Not that he didn't have intellectual worries too, because he did. Before they'd struck oil, he'd feared he and Amber would have to work their way back home to New York. But Amber had come through. Her memory proved accurate and now he'd paid back his depositors and he was on his way to being a millionaire; Amber was one already.

Pop was back on his feet, but spent most of his day supervising. That was fine with Wellman. He needed the man's expertise and didn't want him overdoing. They'd hired men to guard the rigs at night and so far hadn't had any more problems. He still worried—about Amber and the safety of Pop and his crews. The going wage was four dollars a day, but he paid his men four-fifty to make sure he had the best.

Throughout October, the temperature still reached eighty degrees some days. At least it wasn't a hundred. They'd just taken another oil sample on the Lila Simpson Number Three and the results were promising. He walked over to share the news with Pop who was talking with a big man Wellman hadn't seen around. Something about him did look familiar though. He heard Pop say, "Here he comes now."

The man turned and before Wellman could speak, a big fist caught him in the jaw. He fell back with a thud, but quickly regained his feet, fists at the ready. "What the h…. Samuelson, is that you?"

"You know it is, you thieving, lying son-of-a-bitch." The man charged. Wellman sidestepped and Samuelson went down with a roar.

"Just hold on a minute." But a fist landed on his jaw sending him sprawling again." Damn it, he'd had enough. He lurched to his feet, threw a couple of punches, and hit Samuelson on the mouth and nose. Blood spurted, spraying them both. The big man hit the ground. Sprawled in the dirt, he sat shaking his head like a bull and wiped blood off his face. Wellman shook his fist. "Tell me what this is about. I've been sending money to the bank to pay you back. What more do you want?"

Samuelson rose to his feet, murder in his eye. "I want what you promised us, not thirty-five percent."

Wellman was stunned. What was going on here? He didn't believe for a minute that Samuelson was lying to him. If the man said he only got a percentage, that's what he got. "Are you telling me, you didn't receive the full amount I owed you?"

"Damn right, and I'm here to see that you pay me, protect my interests so to speak." His shoulders dropped in defeat. "I'm finding a job and sticking to you like glue."

Something rotten was going on back at the bank and he intended to find out what. "Come on over to the office with me. Let's get to the bottom of this." Samuelson's frown said he didn't quite believe him, but he nodded. Wellman called out to Pop. "I'll be back later. Send someone to the office if you need me."

"Sure thing, son."

By noon, they'd developed a game plan. It was obvious Lancaster was embezzling from the bank and their depositors were the ones paying the price. Of course, the manager could be skimming from other accounts too and from the profits. Wellman shook his head in disgust. He'd been a fool to leave someone else in charge for so long.

He wanted Amber out of Kilgore and this was a good excuse to send her home. She'd run this office and kept their books like the pro she was so he didn't have a doubt in the world she couldn't straighten out Lancaster's mess. Wellman wanted all Lancaster's assets seized and the man in jail.

Amber's face had turned bright red as she listened to Samuelson's story. "That no good piece of thieving trash." She shook her finger at Wellman. "You remember how patronizing he was toward me? I knew then he was conniving. To think I wouldn't understand the bank's books." She snorted. "The jackass."

He resisted the urge to grin at the feisty woman and her choice of word—jackass. She'd called him that on occasion. Yes, she'd see Lancaster in jail and his possessions seized until he could go to trial. His wife was an asset to him and the bank. A sense of regret washed over him. What a shame their partnership couldn't be a permanent one. No need to dwell on what couldn't be. At least they still had more time together. He didn't think Amber would leave for a while and when she decided to file for divorce, it would take at least a year to get one finalized. That gave him time to sort out his feelings. His feelings? He didn't like the direction his mind was taking. He didn't want to feel.

"Amber, I need you to go home and take care of this. Can you do it?"

Her face paled. Was she scared? Surely not. Not his lively wife. "Can't you go? I'd rather stay here."

What was it about not wanting to leave Kilgore? "You know I can't, sweetheart. I'm needed here on the sites."

She nodded, but wouldn't look at him. She reached down and picked up her handbag off the floor. "I better go buy a ticket. It'll take four days to reach New York and there is no time to spare. While I'm gone, you might want to call the FBI and have them shut down the bank and freeze all of Lancaster's assets."

He walked outside with her. "What's wrong, Amber? I know you don't want to leave here, but it can't be helped."

She sighed. "You wouldn't understand. Don't worry, I'll be fine." Before he could reply, she stepped off the sidewalk and started toward the train depot. Heaviness settled in the region of his heart. An inner voice warned him that things would never be the same between them.

~*~

With what felt like desperation, they made love half the night, as if they'd never hold each other again. In her heart, Amber knew they wouldn't. They'd fulfilled their promise to each other and now it was time to move on. She wasn't the wife Wellman wanted. With each touch, Amber memorized the texture of Wellman's skin, his own special smell mixed with Old Spice. His voice, as he cried out in release was locked away in a special chamber of her heart. How long would she be able to pull the memories out and remember before they became too faint to retain?

The following morning, Alva, Pop, and Sarah were there with Wellman to see her off. Wellman walked her to the steps of her passenger car—she'd be traveling first class this time—and held her close for a long time. She breathed in his familiar scent and bit her cheek to keep from crying out loud. He kissed her deeply and she poured her soul into her response.

He released her and his brown eyes devoured her face as if taking a picture in his memory. With his thumbs, he wiped the tears away. "Take care of yourself. Call me if you need me."

She choked out. "I will."

"For God's sake, Amber. Don't look so solemn. It's not like this is forever."

"Isn't it? We agreed when we recouped your fortune we'd divorce. I think we've fulfilled our contract."

"You want a divorce?" It had been a mutual understanding when they first married and now he looked at her like she'd said something foul. His face infused with color. Whether it was anger, embarrassment, or what, she didn't know, but a surge of hope swelled around her heart. Maybe he'd changed his mind.

"Isn't that what you want? You've never said otherwise, that you loved me." Inside she begged him to say no. She longed for the words, *I love you, Amber*, But, they didn't come.

His face, now ashen, lines etched around his mouth and eyes expressionless, gave her no hope. "Yes, that's what I want." He turned and left her standing alone, to climb aboard unassisted. With gaping mouths and worried frowns, their friends turned and watched him leave.

She found her seat and stared out the window at the retreating back of her husband. Her chest was empty, her heart lying on the dusty boardwalk in a hundred pieces.

Eight

"Damn her to hell and back," muttered Wellman. His heart had been broken once before, not to mention his pride, and it damn sure wasn't going to happen again. Let her get her divorce. He didn't need her anymore. She'd made him rich and he was grateful, but gratitude only went so far.

What was the rush? Couldn't she at least wait, until what, until he fell completely in love with her? No, he didn't love her. He liked her, respected her. They had wonderful sex, they had fun together, but that's all they had.

He stomped into the oil office. Samuelson sat behind the desk where Amber had worked. Samuelson had been an accountant before the crash so Wellman felt he could handle the job here. He didn't know why he trusted the man, but he did. And Lord only knows why he should give him a chance after what he'd done to his hand and forcing him and Amber to marry. Hell, maybe he was grateful.

"What's your first name, Samuelson?"

"Robert."

Wellman nodded. "Okay." He sat down in one of the chairs. "You understand all the paperwork so far?"

"Sure do. Don't worry, Mr. Hathaway. If I don't understand something, I'll lock up and come ask. I can't tell you how much I appreciate you hiring me."

"You do that, Robert. And call me Wellman."

His father and Hattie would meet Amber's train when she got in. Wellman had called Howard Lancaster at home the previous evening with the news he needed to check out a bank for sale in San Francisco. Howard had boarded a train for California before the bank opened that morning. When Lancaster arrived, Wellman's banker friend would inform Howard he'd changed his mind about the sale and apologize for wasting his time.

He reached for the phone, called New York, and got the FBI office in New York on the phone. As planned, FBI auditors were at the Hathaway Bank when the doors opened that morning and funds of all employees were locked until their investigation was finished. Hopefully by the time Amber reached New York, the audit would be complete and Lancaster could be arrested when he returned from the west coast.

He left the office and went to check on the Lila Simpson Number Three. The core samples indicated she could produce oil any day now. He should have been excited, but for some reason he wasn't. He snorted. Some reason. Yeah, right. His wife hadn't been gone a minute and he was miserable, doubly so because he regretted his words at the station. He started back across the road

What did she mean he'd never said he loved her? Didn't he show her every time he touched her? And last night, didn't he tell her with his body and soul when they made love? She hadn't told him either, but he knew, he could feel it in everything she did and said. He stopped walking and stood for a minute in the middle of the road. A car honked and he jumped out of the way.

Oh, God. She loved him. Women needed to hear the words more so than men. Why couldn't things have continued like they were? Just taking a day at a time? Would she accept such an arrangement? Hell, women were so much trouble. At least he had time to decide what he wanted. It took over a year to get a divorce in New York.

~*~

Mr. Hathaway and Hattie met Amber's train and quickly hustled her into the Packard. Hattie drove while Amber chatted with the older man in the back seat.

"As soon as I shower and change clothes, I'd like to get to the bank. I'll be sleeping there until this mess is straightened out." She leaned back against the seat and closed her eyes for a moment. "Can I borrow the Packard?"

"Of course you can, but you can't stay there by yourself. It's not safe for a woman alone."

She patted the old man's knee. "I'll be fine." She leaned forward and touched Hattie's shoulder. "Could you get me a pillow and a couple of blankets to take back with me?"

"Of course I can, some towels and wash cloths too. Mr. Wellman often stayed overnight and cleaned up in the bathroom off his office. A shame it hasn't a tub. Will a shower do?" Before Amber could answer, Hattie continued. "I'll pack you a basket of food. Of course, there are several good restaurants nearby, but it will be nice to have food handy if you don't want to go out." Hattie looked back over the seat at her employer. "Now, Mr. Hathaway, this young woman will be just fine. You quit your worrying."

There wasn't a bathroom off the office in her time. It must be the space they used as a storage room. "That'd be perfect, Hattie. Thank you!" Seems Hattie had decided she might like Amber after all.

Early that afternoon, freshly dressed in one of her suits and hats, Amber pulled up in front of the Hathaway Building. Steven ran out and rushed around to open her door. "Mrs. Hathaway, we didn't know to expect you."

"This is a surprise visit, Steven. I have items in the trunk. Bring them upstairs to Mr. Hathaway's office as soon as you can. I'll be staying over."

His mouth gaped. "You mean overnight?"

"Yes. For a while."

The man struggled to not comment, doffed his hat, and rushed to open the door to the bank before parking her car. A gust of wind lifted the brim of Amber's hat. She clapped a hand to the crown to hold it in place and she strode through the entrance to see how the audit progressed.

Security guards stood at the lobby doors checking each person who entered. She removed the documents Wellman had provided from her bag and handed them to the officer who appeared to be in charge. He quickly scanned the papers and returned them to her. "Officer Harrison, Mrs. Hathaway. Let me know if I can help you in any way." He held the glass door for her.

"Thank you, Officer. Let's hope that's not necessary."

The tellers, with business slow and the FBI in their midst, stood behind their windows doing their best to look busy. Nervous smiles flitted across their faces when she entered. "Relax everyone. As soon as a certain matter is resolved we'll be back to business as usual."

A murmur of relief passed through the group. "As soon as the doors are locked at two o'clock, finish up your daily tallies then go to the break room and have a quick cup of coffee. We'll be meeting in the conference room at three sharp." They stared, frozen in place. She clapped her hands twice. "Hop to it. I don't believe any of you are in danger of losing your jobs." They scurried about and rushed to do her bidding.

Constance appeared at her side, brow furrowed. "Is there anything I can do to help, Mrs. Hathaway, er, Amber?"

"Yes, there is. I want to see all the personnel folders upstairs in Wellman's office as soon as possible." Amber laid her hand on the woman's arm. "And Constance, your job isn't in jeopardy either."

The tension on her face eased. "Thank goodness. I couldn't imagine what or if I'd done anything wrong, but one can't help worrying, you know."

Amber smiled. "Yes, I know. I'll be upstairs in ten minutes and would like to have the files by then."

"I'll have them on your desk."

"Thank you. Then round up everyone and have them report to the conference room at three o'clock."

Amber strode to Howard Lancaster's office to find an elderly gentleman, wire-rimmed glasses sitting low on his nose, seated behind the large desk going through a folder. She knew he was an accountant for the FBI. Intent on his work, he didn't hear her enter.

She approached the desk and offered her hand. "Mr. Roland."

He stood and grasped her hand. "Mrs. Hathaway,

it's a pleasure to meet you." He motioned to the chairs. "Have a seat." He sat back down. The leather creaked with his weight. "My team has already uncovered much of the evidence we need to prosecute. The FBI has been in and out. They're satisfied with our findings and will be taking Mr. Lancaster as soon as he returns. It appears no one else was involved, but we're double checking on his secretary, Mrs. Boatman."

That was good news and made her job easier. "I'd like to be here when you arrest him." At that moment Officer Harrison entered with a red-faced Howard Lancaster.

Howard, furious, tried to yank his arm from the security guard's hold. Spittle flew from his mouth as he faced the man behind his desk. "Who are you and what are you doing in my office?"

"I'm Jacob Roland, Mr. Lancaster, an accountant for the FBI. It appears you've been embezzling funds from the Hathaway Bank. We'll be arresting you momentarily."

Howard's blotched face visibly blanched. "What the hell are you talking about?"

"Watch your language, sir, there's a lady present." Officer Harrison's tone brooked no argument.

Lancaster turned and saw her. "Thank God." He looked behind her. "Where is Wellman?"

"He's not coming, Howard. I'm here to take care of this nasty business."

"You can see I'm understandably upset. I return from my trip to find my office and the bank taken over by—" He waved his hand at the officer and Mr. Roland. "—these men threatening arrest."

"That's what happens to people who abuse their

authority as you have, Howard." She'd not liked the man before, but after learning of his deceit, she despised him.

"Surely you don't believe what they're accusing me of?" He took a deep breath to steady himself, but Amber could see the fear in his eyes. "I've done nothing illegal. I've worked hard to bring this bank back to its former prosperity."

"Howard, Howard, you're such a convincing liar."

"How dare you!"

"Guess who came to Kilgore to find us? Robert Samuelson. You remember him, don't you? It seems you've not been paying Mr. Samuelson and the others their full returns. You've been pocketing part of it for yourself."

"I did no such thing. That was handling fees. Money the depositors owed the bank."

"Oh, come off it, Lancaster." Evidently Mr. Roland had heard his fill. "We know you've deposited the money into your private accounts and from the looks of the bank's books, you've skimmed money in other areas. As of this morning, all of your funds have been frozen." He nodded to Amber. "Are you and Mr. Hathaway ready to press charges? If so, they'll keep him in jail until we can finish our audit."

She sneered, "Yes, of course."

He shrieked like a madman as Officer Harrison and another guard hauled him away. Amber shuddered at the glare of hate he shot her.

She hurried upstairs to go through the folders Constance had left on her, well, actually Wellman's desk. Before sitting down, she removed the hat and finger combed her hair. Though she admired the styles of this period, she wasn't used to them. The contraption felt odd on her head. It felt good to let her scalp breathe.

She spent thirty minutes going through the files and made up her mind who would be promoted to Howard's job and how the vacancies left by that action would be filled. She jotted down the names on a piece of paper. If Wellman didn't like how she handled things, he should have come himself, but she believed he'd approve.

Amber picked up her notes, stepped into the hall, and pushed the elevator button. The motor of the device was louder than the hum of modern elevators. James greeted her with a restrained smile. "Which floor is the conference room on, James?"

"Second floor, ma'am. Shall I be taking you there?"

"Yes, please. And James, your job is secure."

A grin split his face. "Praise be." He stepped out into the hall and motioned with a gloved hand. "The conference room is at the end of the hall."

She nodded. "I'd like for you to go get Steven and both of you come to the meeting we're having there."

The group had assembled and sat talking quietly. It was crowded around the table and many stood. When she entered they fell silent. "Constance, is everyone here?" Darn, she needed to remember to call Constance Mrs. Dyer in front of the others.

"Yes."

"What I have to say today will soon be public knowledge. I'd prefer that if possible you'd refrain from gossiping." She let her gaze land on each individual. "Is that understood?"

Heads nodded, accompanied by, "Yes, ma'am."

"This afternoon Howard Lancaster was arrested for embezzling funds from the bank and cheating depositors of part of the repayments due them as promised by Mr. Hathaway."

Gasps echoed around the room.

"The news will hit the papers tomorrow morning. You are not to speak to reporters or give information to anyone about the situation. If I discover you've fed the gossip lines, your job will be terminated. Is that understood?"

All heads nodded, eyes round as they sat rooted to the spot. Thank goodness it was only Thursday so surely they could keep the situation under wraps until the morning. "You will not come to work tomorrow but will receive full pay." Since the FDIC didn't come into being until 1933, they wouldn't be violating Federal laws by closing. She'd have to come up with some excuse to prevent a panic. "Mrs. Dyer, I want you to have painters in here first thing tomorrow morning to repaint the lobby. Also, get someone to check the status and clean if necessary all the marble. I also want someone performing a routine check on the elevators, and plumbers to check the lavatories for leaks." She'd have Steven make a sign informing the public they were closed for one day for maintenance.

"Yes, Mrs. Hathaway. We have a list of people who perform these duties. But someone needs to be here to supervise."

"I'll be here. As a matter of fact, I'll be living upstairs for a few weeks until this situation is resolved."

Now for the part she'd enjoy. "We'll be having several staff changes, promotions actually." She could almost smell the hope emanating off those gathered.

The crash had hurt so many people. She wished she could promote everyone but it wasn't possible.

"Taking over for Mr. Lancaster will be Mrs. Dyer."

A shriek of surprise split the air and Amber couldn't restrain a smile. Constance's hands covered her mouth and her eyes filled with tears. It wasn't common for a woman to assume such a position in this day and time, but Amber planned to alter that.

"Now, we need someone to take over as mine and Mr. Hathaway's secretary. If Mrs. Dyer approves, I'd like for Mrs. Jonas to take that position." Mrs. Jonas was a woman in her fifties who worked as a bookkeeper yet she had a degree from a two-year business college. Unattractive, she'd most likely been passed over for promotion because of her age but her record was immaculate. The woman was visibly crying and those around patted her on the back.

Amber turned her attention to a young man enjoying the success of his fellow workers. He served as a teller but had finished business school. His credentials and work ethic were stellar. "Mr. Paulson." He jerked to attention, his eyes glued to hers. "If you have no objection to being a secretary, and meet with Mrs. Dyer's approval, I'd like for you to be her assistant."

The kid actually "whooped," and the room burst into laughter. His response was a great tension reliever. Blushing, he looked at Constance who grinned and nodded.

Howard's secretary, Mrs. Boatman, sat, hands folded in her lap, face blanched. They had no proof she'd colluded with Howard, but until they knew for sure, her position was on hold.

"Mrs. Boatman, I don't believe you are involved with Mr. Lancaster's illegal activities, but until the auditors exonerate you, your duties will be on hold, with full pay, of course."

Misery lining her face, Mrs. Boatman sobbed. "I understand, Mrs. Hathaway, but promise you I knew nothing about his activities."

Amber felt for the woman. Business was tough, but no one could say she wasn't up to the task. She didn't look forward to meeting with the press tonight but she could handle whatever they threw at her. She could hear the question now.

"What were you thinking promoting a woman to a management position?" They might even question her authority.

Bring it on, boys.

Nine

Wellman choked on his morning coffee. The cup clattered as he set it in the saucer and covered his mouth, choking and gasping for air. Alva pounded him on the back. He raised his hand and managed, "Stop…I'm…okay."

He picked the newspaper up and stared at his wife's face plaster across the front page of the Dallas Morning News. The headline read *Bank Manager at New York's Hathaway Bank Arrested: Woman to Fill Position.* He scanned the article.

"Why, that's Amber." Alva peered over his shoulder as she poured him another cup of coffee. "My, she's a beautiful woman. I bet you miss her."

Hell yes, he did, but he wanted to strangle her right now. What could she have been thinking making Constance bank manager? He sighed and leaned back in his chair. Constance was as qualified as anyone for the job but women just weren't given such powerful positions. In this day and age anyway, especially with the economy as it was. A man should have the job, one with a family to support. He knew at once his line of thinking wasn't fair. Constance may not be married and have children to support, but she did provide for her elderly mother and father.

He finished off his coffee and stood with the paper clutched in his hand. "Thank you for the breakfast,

Alva. Better get by the office before going to the wells."

She winked at him. "Give Amber my love."

He grinned. "I'll do that." More like he'd scorch his wife's ears. She'd been gone only a week and already had put his name into national headlines.

At the office, he sat in Robert's chair and finished reading the article. She'd promoted Mrs. Jonas to the secretary to the president and that skinny young teller as assistant, a fancy name for secretary to the bank manager.

He dropped the paper and stared into space. He couldn't fault her choices. All of those she'd chosen had good credentials. He wondered how she'd gotten David Stiles, his personnel manager, to agree to make Constance manager.

His laugh echoed off the walls. She'd not gotten his approval. Probably hadn't consulted the old man. Wellman bet David had an apoplectic fit when he heard the news.

Wellman lifted the phone and dialed his father's home.

It rang three times before being picked up. "Hathaway residence."

"Hattie, how is Dad?"

"He's doing very well, Mr. Wellman. You know he's crazy about your wife and tickled to death that she's brought that evil man at the bank to justice. You did well in your choice this time, if I may say so."

Hm, that was odd. Amber had won the older woman over pretty fast. "May I speak to her?"

"Why, she's not here. She's been staying at the bank upstairs in your office."

107

In his office? What was she thinking? She had no business staying up there by herself. "Thanks, Hattie. Tell Dad hello." He hung up before she could respond and dialed the bank. It was seven in the morning in New York but he didn't doubt Amber was up.

She picked up on the first ring. "Hathaway Bank, Amber Hathaway speaking."

"Hello, Amber."

"Wellman? How are you?" Amber's heart lodged in her throat. She'd been here three days and the rat was just now calling to see how she was managing.

He laughed but it wasn't a jovial sound. "I almost choked to death on my coffee when I read the headlines this morning."

"Oh? Something shocking on the front page?"

"I'd say so. Your picture and news about a woman being made manager of my bank."

Darn, she'd have loved to see the expression on his face at the news. "Gee, I'll have to run out and get a copy. Is it a good picture of me?"

"Amber, what were you thinking making Constance manager?"

"That she was the most qualified individual for the job. You know it's the truth and times must change, Wellman. I just gave it a little boost." She twirled the phone cord around her finger. "How are you? I'm fine. Thanks for asking." She could hear his breathing on the other end.

"How was your trip?"

"Miserable."

"I'm sorry, but it was necessary. I appreciate your taking care of things there. I assume it will be some months before Howard goes to trial."

"Yes, several months. You'll need to be here to testify in court."

"I'll be there. Just let me know so I can catch the train in plenty of time."

"I'll keep you posted on the FBI's progress."

"Why are you staying at the bank? I don't like it. It's not safe for you. Plus, I know for a fact that sofa's not comfortable."

"I'm fine. James and Steven are taking turns spending the night on a cot in the hallway outside the door." They had deemed themselves her protectors. Both were so insistent she didn't have the heart to order them to stay home. "Was there anything else?"

She waited hoping he'd say he missed her, anything to give her hope.

"No, I guess not."

Struggling to keep her voice steady, she said, "Bye then."

"Amber...I..." Hope rushed to her heart. "Never mind. Bye."

She replaced the handset on the cradle. Her decision was made. That he cared for her, she didn't doubt, but he didn't want her for a wife. As soon as she could concentrate on something other than the bank, she'd file for divorce. People in New York needed an investment banker with inside knowledge on what would produce money in the coming months. She would start her own business and be their source. To hell with Wellman Hathaway.

~*~

Wellman hung up the phone and cursed under his breath. What the hell was wrong with him? Why couldn't he just say it? "I love you, Amber. Stay with me and be my wife." He was a coward, that's why. The phone bounced and the bell tinkled from his resounding blow to the desktop. He rubbed his fist. Damn, he needed a round in the ring to vent his frustrations.

Robert came through the door with a newspaper under his arm, a grin stretching his face. "Got the bastard, didn't we?"

"Yes, we did. Of course it will take a while to see him behind bars, but I promise you it will happen."

"After I realized the whole affair wasn't your doing, I didn't doubt for a minute you'd make it right." He chuckled. "Didn't expect you to be so convincing with your fists."

Wellman grinned. "I don't suppose you'd want to go another round with me. I need to work off some frustration."

"Uh, no, I'll pass. I guess you could go out to the rigs and pick a fight with some of the rowdies."

Wellman shoved the chair back and stood. "What I need is a match in the boxing ring, not a free-for-all." He sighed. "I'll go a few rounds with a sledge hammer."

"You upset with Mrs. Hathaway for giving the manager's job to a woman? It was all the talk in the café this morning."

Great. He'd have the locals voicing their opinions also. Not that other's opinions mattered to him when it came to doing what was right. "Yes and no. Constance Dyers deserves the job and is well-qualified, but it will cause chaos in the business world, especially in New York."

Robert removed his hat and hung it on the hall tree by the door. "Mrs. Hathaway is a smart woman. She wouldn't hire someone who couldn't do the job. I bet my wife and her friends are applauding Mrs. Hathaway right now over their morning tea."

"Yeah, yours and the majority of the women across the country." He shook his head. "I don't know. Maybe it is a good thing, but I bet the Wall Street crowd is going to give her a hard time."

Concern etched Robert's brow. "Will she be able to handle them?"

Wellman laughed. He wished he could be there to watch the show. "Like a pro, Robert, like a pro."

~*~

"Mrs. Hathaway," Mrs. Jonas's voice sounded through the telephone, "Mr. Stiles is here with several gentlemen from banks on Wall Street. They'd like to speak with you." Amber grinned, impressed with the older woman's authoritative tone. "Are you available?"

"Show them to the conference room. I'll be with them shortly." *Shortly, my ass.* She'd let them wait thirty minutes or so. "Offer them a cup of coffee."

Amber hung up and continued viewing the file on her desk. She shut the folder and leaned back in the massive leather chair. Thursday after her announcement in the boardroom, Mr. Stiles voiced his displeasure at not consulting him before making employee changes. After all, hiring and firing was his job. That's what Mr. Hathaway paid him to do. She'd done her best to salve his wounded pride, but he'd have none of it. Perhaps she should have asked his advice but there hadn't been time. Actually, she'd not wanted to consult Stiles because she knew he would object to a woman. She didn't want the hassle of arguing with him.

She checked her appearance in the bathroom

mirror. Her charcoal suit had a pencil thin, mid-calf skirt with a kick pleat in the back. The jacket sported a gored peplum, which emphasized her small waist. She reapplied the Coty red lipstick hating the taste. If she stayed in this time she'd be dead before they developed lipstick that felt creamy on the lips and didn't taste so bad. Heck, it probably had lead in it.

Looking behind each hip, she tried to make sure the seams in her silk stockings were straight. The bathroom needed a full-length mirror. She smoothed her hands down and skirt and exited the room. Passing up the elevator, she took the stairs down to the second floor. A man's heated voice could be heard through the door.

"What is Hathaway thinking to let a woman, especially his wife, handle the affairs of his bank?"

A snort and, "Hell if I know. From her picture in the paper, she's quite a looker. Maybe he's not thinking with his brain. Harharhar."

A round of ribald laughter followed. She didn't wait for them to finish, but waltzed through the door into the haze of cigar smoke.

"Gentlemen." They stood, albeit it reluctantly.

"Mrs. Hathaway." Mr. Stiles and two of her guests had the good grace to blush while the third, chin tucked towards his stocky chest stared belligerently. They had to know she'd heard their comments.

She advanced into the room and went immediately to open the windows. A cross breeze drifted through the room dissipating some of the smoke. In her opinion, cigars stunk like cow poop. She wrinkled her nose and all of the men but Mr. Stocky Body snuffed them out in the ashtrays.

Taking the seat at the head of the table, she waved her hand towards the other chairs. "Sit down gentlemen. I'm delighted you've come to meet me today and welcome me to the banking community."

Ten

Amber coughed and struggled to not laugh out loud. Mr. Stocky Body choked on a mouthful of cigar smoke. David pounded him on the back, and then rushed to the sideboard for a glass of water. "Here, Mr. Stockman, maybe this will help." *Mr. Stockman? How appropriate. The name fit him perfectly.*

Wheezing, gasping for air, Mr. Stockman took the glass of water with a shaking hand and raised it to his lips. After an experimental sip, he took several more but continued to wheeze. From experience at sucking something down the windpipe, Amber knew it would take a few minutes for him to recover.

"Mr. Stiles, while Mr. Stockman regains control, introduce me to the other gentlemen."

He stood. "Directly to your right is Mr. John Knowles, President of First New York Charter Bank and next to him is Mr. Charles Worth, President of Manhattan Bank and Trust."

Amber leaned forward in her chair and shook each man's hand. "It's a pleasure to meet you, gentlemen. That your banks survived the stock market disaster is indicative of your financial and intellectual prowess." Not really, but stroking their egos a little wouldn't hurt anything. Both men sat a little straighter in their chairs and smiled before glancing at Mr. Stockman to observe his reaction.

She turned to Mr. Stockman and offered her hand. "Can we get you anything, Mr. Stockman?" He wiped his big paw on his handkerchief and took her small one, squeezing a bit harder than necessary. She didn't flinch.

"No, thank you, Mrs. Hathaway." His coughing fit hadn't softened his booming baritone. He cleared his throat. "We're here to help you with business matters while your husband is out of the state."

"That's kind of you, but I'm quite able to manage on my own."

"Now, my dear, your announcement of last week is proof you are not. A woman doesn't have the business acumen or the toughness necessary to manage a bank. Why, Mr. Stiles here is bewildered by your promotions and the fact that you didn't consult him is another indication of your needing our help." He waved his now unlit cigar. "We'll help you reverse those untimely decisions and set things right."

Amber couldn't believe the audacity of the big man. Well, of him and his cohorts. She tried to tamp down her anger. They weren't insulting her personally, but the entire female race, a common occurrence in this time period when it came to women in business. Elbows against her waist, hands clasped, she looked at each man in turn, ending with Mr. Stockman.

"That's very considerate of you, but not necessary."

Mr. Stiles started to speak, but she raised a finger and glared. He shut up.

"Mr. Stockman, first of all, I'm not your or anyone's *dear*." The big man's mouth fell open. She cocked an eyebrow and smiled. "Except Mr. Hathaway's, of course. Secondly, though you gentlemen have a number of years on me, I'm just as qualified as you are—maybe more so. I have an MBA from Harvard and have worked as an investment banker for years."

Stockman snorted. "I seriously doubt that. Women aren't accepted into Harvard's MBA program."

Oops, I should've kept my mouth shut on that little boast. Women weren't allowed into the MBA program until 1959.

"Believe what you will, but I'm as qualified as you are. Wellman knows it and trusts me with this bank and to handle his investments. As a matter of fact, you'd be wise to allow me to help you select new venture possibilities for your banks."

"Now, see here, young woman. You'd do well to show some respect." Ah, Mr. Worth speaks.

Mr. Knowles added, "That's right, Mrs. Hathaway. We came here to help, not to be insulted."

Teeth clamped on his cigar, Mr. Stockman grinned. He removed the stogie and muttered, "Well said, gentlemen."

"Isn't that what you've done to me, been disrespectful?"

"Why no, my dear…er, ah, Mrs. Hathaway, we came here with the best intentions." Mr. Stockman placed the cigar in the ashtray and folded his hands on the tabletop. "You've made a mistake in promoting a woman to a management position. The promotion must be rescinded. It sends the wrong message about the banking industry."

"I tried to tell you, Mrs. Hathaway. Women aren't up to high-pressure jobs. Hathaway Bank is unusual in that it hires more women than is standard, but only as secretaries and bookkeepers." Yes, Amber knew the statistics. After World War One—or The Great War, as people in this age would call it—women moved into secretarial and sales jobs in department stores, "lace collar" jobs. Prior to that time they worked as domestics. The only professional jobs they held were in nursing and teaching. At least women were no longer barred from jobs after marriage.

"Yes, Mr. Stiles, I'm aware of that. However, Mrs. Dyers has a college education, she knows the business, Mr. Hathaway trusts her and I trust her. Mr. Hathaway wasn't pleased I'd promoted Mrs. Dyers, but he agreed she was qualified and bowed to my judgment." She stood. "And that is the end of the matter. Now, is there anything else?" She waited. "Nothing? Good day then and please, stop in again."

Mr. Stiles, trying to go unnoticed, slunk to the door and held it open. In a huff, Mr. Stockman, blustering something under his breath about, "you'll change your tune…" stalked out the door with his two associates on his heels.

Amber's days were busy helping Constance settle into her job and trying to adjust to twentieth-century technology. At least they had Electromatic Typewriters and Burroughs's Portable adding machines, not that in her supervisory position she had to use them much, but what she wouldn't do for a laptop computer. Heck, she'd be thrilled with an ancient PC.

Mrs. Boatman was cleared of any wrong doing in Lancaster's scheme and Amber put her to work training Mr. Paulson in his duties as Constance's secretary. She also eased Mrs. Jonas's load as she settled into her new job. Amber would have to find Mrs. Boatman a permanent position soon.

Staying overnight in the office grew tiresome. She didn't want to make the drive to the Hathaway Estate every day, plus she didn't want Mr. Hathaway to grow too attached. He'd wormed his way into her heart. At least she'd still be able to visit him on occasion after the divorce.

The last week of October, Amber started looking at apartments. Her realtor, Mr. Tillman, eager for a sale in such drastic times, came to her office just before closing time with a list of properties for her to browse. Young, dressed in a suit and tie, he took the cup of coffee Mrs. Jonas offered him. When she'd finished her perusal, he placed his empty cup on the serving tray and asked, "Will Mr. Hathaway be joining us?"

"No, he's still in Texas." Amber smoothed her hair in front of the mirror over the credenza.

She liked the new style she'd received at Macy's on Saturday. Mona, the stylist who'd done her hair before leaving for Texas, recognized her and whizzed her toward her station. Amber had been wearing it long, pulled back on the sides with combs. Mona cut it to just above her shoulders, put what she called 'finger wave solution' on it and with Bobbie pins, made waves all over her head. Behind her ears, at the base of her head, Mona placed a million tiny pin curls. Amber gaped at her reflection in the mirror horrified at the possibility of what'd she look like after her hair dried. The stylist patted her shoulders. "Trust me, madam, it's going to look fabulous." She'd been right. After she'd combed it out, full waves tapered down to soft curls that stopped just above Amber's shoulders.

Amber slipped the snood on her head pleased with

how it framed her face and accentuated her hairstyle. She found herself liking the style of the 1930s more every day. The 1930s? It would soon be 1932. She'd been in this time period for over a year now. It didn't seem possible.

"Ah well," Mr. Tillman said, "as long as he's here to sign the papers for the loan, there's not a problem."

She turned to face Mr. Tillman. "Mr. Hathaway won't be here to sign the papers. I'm buying this apartment on my own. I assure you I can afford it. The title will be in my name."

"Mrs. Hathaway, it's impossible to get a loan without your husband's signature."

A week later Amber signed the papers on a three-bedroom apartment three blocks away from the bank. Rather than having Wellman sign a loan, she'd paid cash. The title was in her name. The cost, though considerable in 1930, was a mere pittance to what it would have been in modern time. Plus, the vendor was anxious to sell and Amber didn't quibble on the price. The large living room windows looked out on a scenic park across the street. Amber loved the rich wood floors, well-maintained birds eye maple furniture, chrome accessories, and colored glass of the fully furnished, Art Deco style apartment. She settled in the following weekend and started adding personal touches. Now she had a place of her own.

She spent Thanksgiving weekend with Mr. Hathaway senior at his estate. His cook prepared a big lunch and she and the elderly man played chess after dinner. During the day, she walked in the woods on the estate, enjoying the outdoor air and exercise. Wellman called. Their visit was short, filled with uninteresting facts about the bank, the oil wells, and Kilgore. Nothing personal passed between them other than how are you, how is business at the bank? His call left her depressed.

"What's going on between you and my son?" Amber's hand froze on her rook and she looked up from the chessboard. "And don't lie to me. I heard you on the phone and I can see the despair on your face."

She removed her hand and sat back in the leather wing chair. A fire blazed in the hearth and drew her eyes making her wish she felt as cheery as the blaze felt. She returned her gaze to Mr. Hathaway, his bushy white eyebrows furrowed with concern. "Wellman explained to you how we'd come to be married the night he brought me home. Our marriage isn't permanent. I'll be filing for divorce soon."

"Why?"

"Because he doesn't want me for a wife. He wants a society woman."

"Harrumph! The boy doesn't know what he wants." He shook his finger at her. "Even before you left for Texas, I saw how the two of you looked at the other on the sly. You love him, don't you?"

She brushed a tear off her cheek. "Yes, I do, but love alone can't make a marriage work. I'm the wrong woman for him."

"Nonsense! You're the perfect woman for him, just what he needs." He shook his head. "Madeline never loved him. She's a cold fish. I'm glad they didn't have children. Can't imagine her squeezing a baby, much less an ounce of affection out of that skinny body."

Amber tried not to laugh, but failed. What an expression coming from this old man. The giggles rolled from her. Tears ran down her face and she wiped at them with the handkerchief Mr. Hathaway handed her. "Oh my, I met Madeline you know."

"Really? When?"

"At Macy's before we left for Kilgore. Our marriage shocked her. Evidently she didn't think Wellman capable of caring for anyone other than her." Amber leaned forward and patted his hand. "I put on a good show for her. Wellman caught on and joined me. We left her with her mouth hanging open."

He grinned, and rubbed his hands together in glee. "Wish I could have seen that. She's a snooty bitch."

"Mr. Hathaway. Such colorful language coming from a refined gentleman like yourself."

He snorted. "She's just lucky I didn't tell her how I felt to her face. Of course, I don't doubt she knew." His expression turned serious and he shook a finger at her. "You wait until I finish with that boy. I'll set him straight."

She grabbed his hand. "No, please, don't. Promise me you won't say anything to him about what we discussed today. He'll find out soon enough. After all, it takes a year to get a divorce. If he wants to do anything, talk me out of it, he'll have plenty of time."

She had no intention of waiting a year for a divorce. After studying the divorce laws of New York, she had two choices. She could fly to Havana and set up residency for three months, a tempting opportunity, as she'd love to see Cuba. Or, she could take a train to Reno and live for six weeks. With no desire to get on a 1930s plane after her "barn storming" experience, especially over open water, she opted to take a train to Reno. Rather than make reservations at one of the Dude Ranches in the area known for catering to rich women obtaining divorces, she booked a small suite at the Riverside Hotel. Though it also catered to the divorce clientele, she planned to remain incognito if possible.

Wellman most likely wouldn't come home for Christmas, so she planned to leave the middle of December. Her divorce would be final shortly after the New Year. The bank was running smoothly. If she was needed, she could be reached by phone or, if necessary, she'd fly back to New York for a couple of days to take care of things. Nah, she'd call Wellman and tell him to take care of it. He'd have to replace her soon enough anyway. She had plans for a business of her own.

Eleven

Wellman missed Amber. Not just in bed, but he longed to hear her laugh, to share his ideas and hear her opinions, and look at her across the table while he drank his coffee. It was all he could do not to get on a plane and fly to New York. But he was needed here. Pop was a good supervisor, but if trouble broke out, he wasn't able to knock heads. Wellman had his eye on one of the men who'd been with them awhile, one who'd be able to handle the men if fights erupted. Pete worked hard. He had a wife and child to provide for. Family men tended to be more dependable workers, as they didn't spend time at the Roadhouse drinking at night.

He'd bought a truck and enjoyed riding around the east Texas countryside. Kilgore, with its flatness was so foreign to what he knew in New York. Not that he considered it ugly, he didn't. It was just different. Alva had been so good to them. Yes, they'd paid her the going rate for a room, but she'd become more than just their landlady. She worked hard. He noticed how swollen her legs were everyday when he came in to eat, yet she insisted on cooking for him. On occasion he convinced her to go out with him to the café.

As a surprise, he hired a group of men to build a row of three small cabins at the back of Alva's property. The woman wouldn't accept money from him but Wellman wanted her to have a means of income and quit her job at the cotton gin. So, he'd begun construction on the cottages before she could argue. Teary eyed, she'd hugged him when he'd moved into the house he'd built for himself and Amber, and voice shaky, added, "I can't thank you enough. You're the closest thing I have to a son."

Wellman patted her back and kissed the top of her silver gray head. "If my mother had lived, I know she'd have been just like you."

She sniffed. "I'll miss cooking for you, my boy."

"I didn't say I wouldn't be over for dinner on occasion."

Wellman could still hear her laugh of delight.

His house, situated on fifteen acres several miles outside of town, was almost finished. It had four bedrooms and two bathrooms upstairs, and a bath, large family kitchen, and living room downstairs. With a wide porch all around, it was a typical farm house, just a little bigger and nicer than most. He couldn't wait for Amber to see it. He was a fool for not calling her, telling her he loved her. After the New Year, when the weather was bad and work slow, he'd make the trip and set things right between them. While in the city, he'd hire someone to serve as President of the bank when they couldn't be there.

December 12, 1931 turned nippy. For some reason, cold weather in east Texas caused more misery than it did in New York. He didn't know why, but it might have to do with the humidity. Wellman pulled his coat up around his ears against the cold wind. The radio said it was 32 degrees. He ducked into Nathan's Jewelry Shop. He and Amber had been married a year and a half. Fool that he was he'd not bought her a wedding ring. No wonder she thought he wanted a divorce. But, a man couldn't send a woman a wedding ring through the mail. A ring should be given in person. He looked through the glass cases and his eyes lit on a diamond broach in the shape of an airplane. He wondered if she'd understand its significance? The Fourth of July picnic and the barnstorming. Nathan wrapped it in festive paper and promised to have it in the mail before noon.

Wellman walked to the office, his step lighter than it had been earlier, pleased with Amber's gift. He opened the door to find Robert on the phone. "Hold on Mr. Hathaway, he just walked in."

Wellman laid his hat on the desk and took the phone. "Hello Father. How are you?"

"I'm good. What about you? When are you coming home? You're needed here, you know." A hint of dread touched Wellman at his father's weak voice.

"You're not sick are you? You sound congested."

"Nothing but a cold. Don't you start harping. Hattie's fussed over me for a week so don't you start in. Even called Amber to come out and coddle me."

Wellman sagged with relief. "I'm glad you're being looked after. How are Hattie and Amber?"

"Hattie's fine. Don't know about Amber. She mopes around, takes long walks in the cold. Acts depressed if you ask me. Sure looks pretty though. Has a new hairstyle and has bought some new suits." He chuckled. "She calls them her 'power suits.' Ever heard of such a thing?"

"No, I haven't. Must be one of her expressions from the future."

"I expect so. She bought a big, fancy apartment just three blocks from the bank. And her own Packard. Rented office space a block away from the bank to start an investment company. She's not a woman to stand still very long, if you know what I mean."

An apartment? Why would she do that? He'd always thought about having a place in the city but kept putting off looking. His heart raced. Dread crept through his system. Was she planning her life without him? It was evident she wasn't sitting around waiting on him to support her.

"You better make up your mind what you want in life, son. We don't always get a second chance." Wellman heard muffled coughing, evidently Father had covered the mouthpiece.

He heard Hattie's voice in the background. "Tell him she loves him."

And a hushed, "Quiet, old woman." Then, loud and clear, "That's all I'm going to say on the subject. Bye, my boy."

Wellman replaced the handset. Amber bought an apartment. The situation appeared worse than he'd thought. He grabbed his hat and headed for the door. "If anyone calls for me I'll be at one of the sites, Robert. I'll check back in around five."

"I'll tell them, Wellman."

Wellman found Pop at the Daisy Bradford #1. "Pop, I need to go home for Christmas, if possible."

"Well, of course you do, son. You need to see that pretty wife of yours." The old man grinned like a fool and wiggled his eyebrows. Wellman couldn't restrain a chuckle. "You go on. We'll be fine."

"I don't want to leave you alone. What if a fight

breaks out? You need some backup." Wellman didn't want to say he feared the man would be hurt again.

"What's your opinion of Pete?"

Pop scratched his bewhiskered chin. "Why you asking?"

"With me going home for a week or so, I want you to have someone to help you keep the wells running smoothly. You can't work twenty-four hours a day."

"He's a good worker. Tough. If you put him over the men, some that's been here longer are gonna cause trouble."

"I expect as much. You think he can handle it?"

"With fists as big as his, I bet he can handle whatever gets in his way."

"Yeah, me too."

Wellman approached Pete just before lunch. The man, pleased with the extra dollar a day and the opportunity to prove himself, agreed to take on the job. Wellman announced Pete's promotion on the spot. By dinner Pete had been in three fights, coming out on top all three times. He didn't boast about his victories, just spit in the dust, slapped his hat back on his head, and went back to work. Things would be fine. Wellman had chosen well.

Wellman purchased his train ticket scheduled to leave Kilgore December eighteenth arriving in New York on the twenty-third. Neither his father nor Amber knew he was coming. He wanted it to be a surprise. At two o'clock in the morning of the eighteenth, loud pounding woke him. It was Pete. The Lila Simpson Number Three had finally come in.

His trip would have to wait.

~*~

Amber sat on the Boeing 80 at Newark Airport waiting for takeoff. She'd been unable to get a direct train to Reno so decided to show a little courage and fly. The engines were loud, so unlike the jets to which she was accustomed. She concentrated on the activities of the female flight attendants or air stewardesses as they were called. Boeing was the only airline to date to use women in this role and the fact that they were nurses added to their credibility.

At least the Boeing had forced-air ventilation. Opening a window for exposure to fresh air didn't sit well with her. Though they wouldn't fly high enough to escape all turbulence Amber felt she'd be able to manage. She'd never been airsick, carsick, or seasick. Hopefully today would be no different. When they were finally underway, the plane climbed and dropped, and then climbed again. When it at last settled at a constant altitude, Amber released her grip on the armrest, closed her eyes, and tried to rest. The noise made sleeping impossible. It didn't bother some passengers. The man beside her slept soundly, his snores barely audible over the hum of the engines.

As they deplaned at Hubbard Field and stepped on to the tarmac, several photographers stood ready and snapped each passenger's picture. Amber raised her large clutch bag in front of her face just as the bulb flashed. She didn't relish being included in a gossip column for the rich and famous divorce seekers. Since Nevada's new divorce law requiring only a six-week residency, the Reno area catered to those from other states seeking to dissolve their marriages.

Just inside the airport terminal, a man in uniform approached her. "May I drive you to your destination, madam?"

"Yes, thank you." She handed him her luggage tickets and he collected her bags and loaded them into his cab.

"Where to?"

"The Riverside Hotel." She hoped she'd made the right decision when passing on the Dude Ranches. The thought of horseback riding and sunning by the pool had been tempting, but it was a more relaxed environment and the idea of constant contact with others didn't appeal to her. The Riverside was as well known, but she'd be in the city and could explore. Who knows, she might decide on a gambling venture.

Her lawyer had told her that the majority of individuals seeking divorce were cast-off women in Reno on the orders of their husbands. Amber shuddered at the ruthlessness of these men and the dire situations of the women who'd probably struggle for the remainder of their lives to make ends meet while their exes lived lavish lifestyles.

Money certainly wasn't everything, but a woman with her own could provide for herself and not be at the mercy of a man. Amber didn't intend to be under any man's thumb when it came to money or any other aspect of life. What was she thinking? Many men treated their wives fairly when it came to divorce. Guilt nagged at her for not telling Wellman her intentions. Was she the one being unfair?

At the hotel, she registered under her middle and maiden name, Elizabeth Mathis. The desk clerk handed her a sealed message. She tore the envelope open to find a note from her Reno lawyer indicating he'd received her documents from her New York attorney and arrangements for her divorce were underway. She'd wired a hundred dollars to the man. That's all it took to dissolve a marriage. Of course, that was a lot of money in 1931.

A bellman took her luggage and escorted her upstairs to her suite of rooms. Oh she loved the personal service of the 1930s. Fresh flowers sat on the entry hall table as well as in the living room and bedroom. Double windows in both rooms overlooked a beautiful segment of the Truckee River. It'd be a lovely view to enjoy over breakfast.

A maid appeared and started unpacking her clothes. "May I draw you a bath, Miss Mathis?"

"That would be lovely. Thank you."

"My pleasure. It'll be ready in five minutes."

Amber kicked off her heels and sat on the sofa to browse through the paper while she waited. A half page article on the bottom of the front page caught her eye.

Kilgore, Texas: The Lila Simpson #3 Blows. Oil gushes in at 15,000 barrels a day.

Amber breathed a sigh of relief. She'd accomplished what she'd promised to do for Wellman. With her knowledge of the past, she'd provided him a way back to his former financial security.

For herself, Amber had a purpose. Rather than try to return to her time, she'd stay in 1930 and help people invest and recoup their fortunes. It wouldn't be easy staying in New York, seeing Wellman from time to time, loving him as she did, but modern time held nothing for her.

Twelve

Wellman boarded the train in Kilgore on February 1, 1932. His private compartment, with private bath, was a far cry from the sleeper car he and Amber had shared with so many others on their trip to Kilgore. That her predictions proved true, that they were now wealthy, still amazed him. He was grateful, not just for the fact he'd recouped his and his father's personal wealth, but because he'd been able to repay his depositors.

His heart thumped in anticipation of seeing Amber. He'd tried to call her on Christmas Day to wish her a Merry Christmas, but Father said she was out of town. "All I know is she said she'd be out of town for over a month. She's your wife. If you'd been tending to business you'd know where she'd gone."

Father was right. He'd put off dealing with the issue of telling his wife how he felt, and now he might pay for his procrastination. Amber could be off somewhere with another man. The possibility made his gut twist. It was too horrible to contemplate. Could he have already lost her? No, he wouldn't think along those lines. Amber wouldn't be with another man without divorcing him first. Of that he was sure.

He slipped into his suit coat and straightened his tie in the mirror attached to the door. The dress clothes felt foreign on his body, confining after so much time in work clothes. He walked to the dining car. A bar held a variety of area newspapers. He grabbed a copy of The Dallas Morning News and found a table. A waiter in white coat appeared to take his order.

Flipping open the paper, he scanned the front-page headlines. Unemployment was up to 24.1 percent. A picture showed scores of men lined up waiting for a chance at a job. For those lucky enough to be hired, the average wage for a year was one thousand, six hundred fifty dollars. The price of a new home was six thousand, five hundred ten. Wellman shook his head. It was a difficult time. People were living on the streets and in old cars.

He turned the page and Amber's face stared back at him from under a small brimmed hat. What the hell…? He drew the paper closer to read the caption. *Elizabeth Mathis, resident of Riverside Hotel, looks amazingly like Amber Hathaway, wife of banker and oil magnate Wellman Hathaway. Could the beautiful Mrs. Hathaway be in Reno to take advantage of Reno's six weeks divorce?*

A Reno divorce? He let the paper drop to the table and leaned back in his chair. He blew out a deep breath of air. Losing her was what he deserved. Disgusted with himself and sick at heart, he shoved his chair back and strode with purpose to the end of the train where he could stand in the cold air and watch the Texas landscape rush by.

He was a fool. He'd let his bad experience with Madeline affect his thinking. She'd been the society wife he believed he'd wanted, the perfect mother for his children. If they'd had children, she'd have been a terrible mother. Amber would be a wonderful mother.

She was full of love and life.

When had his outlook on marriage and family changed? The moment he'd fallen in love with his wife. And now they were divorced.

Maybe this was the best way.

~*~

Amber stood at the window in her apartment. She fingered the diamond pin attached to her dress. Reminiscent of their picnic last July, it had been a Christmas gift from Wellman. A thoughtful one. She glanced down, turning the small plane to watch it sparkle. The glitter reminded her of stars.

She stared out at the lights of Manhattan's skyline. Many nights, after work, she curled up on the sofa and drew comfort from the scenic view. Time and again she asked herself the same question—had she done the right thing in filing for divorce out of state without Wellman's knowledge? Fair or not, what did it matter? He'd wanted a divorce so she gotten one. He'd been home several weeks now and tonight they'd see each other for the first time in four months. That fact spoke volumes.

The doorbell rang. Her heart thumped in response. It was time. She strode across the thick carpet covering a portion of the beautiful wood floors. Her heels clicked against the marble tile in the entryway. Before opening the door, she glanced at her hair in the hall mirror and smoothed her hands down the skirt of her long emerald green dress. She'd not known what to wear but decided on the formal attire she remembered seeing worn so much in movies of the 1930s.

Taking a deep breath, she pasted a smile on her face and opened the door. Wellman stood, hat in his hand, looking more handsome than she'd ever seen him. Or maybe it was because she'd not seen him for so long. Fit and tan from working outdoors, his suit coat emphasized broad shoulders that tapered to a narrow waist and hips. He smiled as he studied her, gaze resting for a significant moment on the pin. His gray eyes drew her and she couldn't look away. "Hello, Amber. You look lovely. Dad said you had a new hairstyle. It becomes you."

"Thank you." She stepped back. "Please come in. You look well." She took his hat and placed it on the hall table. "Can I get you something to drink?"

"No, thank you." He looked around the room as they entered the living area. "This is very nice. You have a wonderful view of Manhattan." He let his hand run along the back of the soft peach colored velvet sofa. "The décor suits you."

She motioned toward the stuffed dove gray leather chair adjacent to the sofa. "Have a seat. How are things in Kilgore?"

He sat in the chair and placed his hands on the arms, thumbs stroking the fabric. "The wells are producing nicely. Everyone said to tell you hello. Of course, they have no idea I'll be returning a divorced man or that they'll never see you again."

"Yes, well…" She shrugged. What could she say? Still standing, she strode to the secretary and retrieved a copy of the divorce decree and handed it to him. "Here's a copy for your records."

Wellman took the paper, and without glancing at it put it inside his suit coat pocket. "I guess it's settled then."

Her heart sank. He'd accepted the divorce without

even a rebuke at her going out of state to obtain it. She nodded. "Yes, I expect so."

"Sit down, please. I have something to say."

Oh dear, she wasn't up for this. He needed to go home so she could have a good cry. Struggling to maintain her dignity and not show how crushed she was, she sank onto the peach colored velvet sofa to the left of his chair.

"What are your plans for the future?"

"I've opened an office and will be advising individuals on investments. That, with my share of income from the wells, should allow me to live comfortably." Her standard of living today would far exceed that of what she'd been accustomed to in the future.

Brow furrowed, he studied her face as if looking for clues. "You don't plan to try to get back to your time period, to the future?"

"No, there is nothing for me there, even if it were possible, which I doubt. My arriving here was a strange accident, unlikely to be repeated. Here I'm needed. Plus, I find it fascinating to check on my grandmother once in a while. I don't want to interfere with her life or confuse history, but seeing her on occasion is nice." *And her parents. She'd figure out some way to see them too. For the first time she wondered if she'd be born in 1982. Or would another child be born in her place. Only time would tell.*

He nodded. "I'm surprised you'd want to stay."

She shrugged. "Yes, me too. But I've made up my mind."

Wellman cleared his throat. "I really messed things up, didn't I?"

"What are you talking about?"

"I love you, Amber. I could kick myself for not telling you long ago, before you left Kilgore, but I was stubborn and unreasonable. Plus, I got mad when you mentioned divorce because I thought that's what you wanted. I should have at least fought to keep you."

Hope blossomed in Amber's chest. "You love me?"

"Yes, more than I can say."

Voice cracking with grief and regret, she added, "You love me, but don't want to be married to me, for me to have your children." She shook her head. "That's a strange kind of love, Wellman."

"I had dim-witted ideas, didn't want to love again. Yes, I wanted a wife, one I could respect but not fall in love with." He scoffed. "Pretty stupid, huh?"

"Yes, I'd say so, but we all have our hang-ups."

His head bobbed and he grinned. "Is hang-ups another of your words from the future? Father told me about your power suits." He cleared his throat but it didn't clear the gruffness from his voice. "How do you feel about me, Amber?"

She wouldn't lie. It'd serve no purpose. "I love you. I've loved you since shortly after we married."

"Thank God." He took her hand in his large, work-worn one. With his thumb, he stroked her knuckles. "Can you forgive me for causing you worry and pain the past four months?"

Rolling her lips inward to keep from crying, she struggled to control her voice. When she could speak, she said, "I forgive you, Wellman, and wish you much happiness in life."

"I'm glad we're divorced. We were forced into

marriage. Now we can start over and marry because we love each other." He dropped to one knee and removed a ring box from his coat pocket. He flipped it open to reveal a large diamond set in a white gold mounting surrounded by smaller stones.

She gasped with surprise and the tears she'd tried to keep at bay trailed down her cheeks. Were those tears in his eyes or was her vision blurred from her own?

"I love you Amber. I want to live with you the rest of my life, have children with you. Will you marry me?"

Heart lodged in her throat, she sniffed and managed to squeak, "Yes."

Linda LaRoque

About the Author

Linda LaRoque is a Texas girl, but the first time she got on a horse, it tossed her in the road dislocating her right shoulder. Forty years passed before she got on another, but it was older, slower, and she was wiser. Plus, her students looked on and it was important to save face.

A retired teacher who loves West Texas, its flora and fauna, and its people, Linda's stories paint pictures of life, love, and learning set against the raw landscape of ranches and rural communities in Texas and the Midwest. She is a member of RWA, her local chapter of HOTRWA, NTRWA and Texas Mountain Trail Writers.

Linda writes contemporary western romances, time travel historical romances, women's fiction and futuristic romances.

~ * ~

Visit Linda at these locations:
www.lindalaroque.com
http://www.lindalaroqueauthor.blogspot.com
www.lindalaroque.com
https://www.facebook.com/linda.laroque
http://www.goodreads.com/author/show/649259.Linda_
LaRoque

Other Books by Linda LaRoque